W9-AHM-444

THE
SHOGUN'S
GOLD

THE
SHOGUN'S
GOLD

A Novel of 19TH-Century Financial Intrigue

MASAYOSHI SATO

TRANSLATED BY MARK SCHILLING

KODANSHA INTERNATIONAL
Tokyo • New York • London

Originally published in Japanese as *Taikun no tsūka.*

Copyright © 1991 by Masayoshi Satō

Distributed in the United States by Kodansha America, Inc., 114
Fifth Avenue, New York, N.Y., 10011, and in the United Kingdom
and continental Europe by Kodansha Europe Ltd., Gillingham
House, 38-44 Gillingham Street, London SW1V 1HU. Published by
Kodansha International Ltd., 17-14 Otowa 1-chome, Bunkyo-ku,
Tokyo 112, and kodansha America Inc. All rights reserved. Printed
in Japan.

First edition, 1991
91 92 93 94 10 9 8 7 6 5 4 3 2 1

Library of Congress Cataloging-in-Publication Data

Satō, Masayoshi. 1941-
    [Taikun no tsūka. English]
    The Shogun's gold : a novel of 19th-century financial intrigue /
Masayoshi Sato ; translated by Mark Schilling.—1st ed.
       p.   cm.
    Translation of: Taikun no tsūka.
    ISBN 4-7700-1480-5
    I. Title.
PL861.A838T3513   1991
895.6'3.5—dc20   90-25011
                                         CIP

Translator's Note

Historical novels are common enough: dozens of new ones (and a few fine ones) pour from the presses every year. *Economic* historical novels are another matter. Writers love to weave romances around the wars of nations—not their exchange rates. In the case of Japan, however, the drama of emergence from two-and-a-half centuries of national isolation was very much an economic one. In the Edo (now Tokyo) of 1859 exchange rates were not arcane figures that only the experts claimed to understand, but symbols of a new relationship with the world. In setting them, the Japanese authorities and foreign diplomats uncovered fundamental problems—and unleashed fundamental passions.

It is those problems and passions that concern Masayoshi Sato in *The Shogun's Gold*. Interestingly, he chooses to view them mainly through the eyes of Rutherford Alcock, Britain's first consul general to Japan. This choice has its logic: Alcock played a central role in the tragicomedy of misunderstanding and missed opportunities that plunged Japan into a decade of economic upheaval and political chaos. It also has its dangers; an author who makes his protagonist a foreigner from another century and from a radically different culture is taking a large, almost impossible leap of the imagination.

Mr. Sato, however, has not invented Alcock and his other characters so much as imaginatively revived them through painstaking research in primary source materials, a huge abundance of which exist. Nearly every foreigner in Japan at the time was a potential author, gathering material for a book that would explain this mysterious country to the world. Alcock was among the most zealous and thorough, writing reams of dispatches and notes that would later become the basis for his magnum opus, *The Capital of the Tycoon.*

In the process of sifting through period documents, Sato unearthed a fascinating tale of greed and deception—and presented it in the form of a true detective story that may well stir up new debate about an American diplomatic hero.

But, more importantly, he has traced the tangled web of Japan's relations with its western trading partners to its starting point, and shed light on the causes of our present difficulties. Japan may have long ago lost its financial innocence, but its view of the outside world—and its ways of dealing with it—have strong roots which were already sunk deep when Rutherford Alcock caught his first, rain-dimmed glimpse of Nagasaki harbor in 1859.

THE
SHOGUN'S
GOLD

*E*uropeans first heard of Japan through Marco Polo, when, at the end of the thirteenth century, he tantalizingly described it (based on Chinese accounts) in his Travels as having "gold in great abundance." When Christopher Columbus was inspired by the Travels to seek this fabled land in 1492, he encountered the Americas instead, and Japan remained a mystery to Europeans.

The first Europeans to visit Japan were the Portuguese, when a group of sailors landed at Tanegashima, a small island to the south of the main Japanese archipelago, in 1543. Japan at that time was in the midst of its Warring States Period—a century-long internal power struggle. Through the Portuguese the Japanese were introduced to firearms, which they copied, improved, and began to manufacture for themselves. These weapons later played a major role in the country's civil wars.

During this time, Japan was one of the leading producers of gold and silver in the world. Following that first visit, Europeans, primarily the Portuguese, rushed to Japan, excited by reports of riches. Christian missionaries came too, mainly Jesuits who proselytized enthusiastically all over the country and won many Japanese converts to the new foreign religion.

The Warring States Period ended in 1600 with the decisive Battle of Sekigahara, which determined the direction Japan was to take for the next 250 years. The victor was the seasoned warlord Tokugawa Ieyasu, who soon established his hegemony over the entire nation. Thus began the Edo Period.

This period was named for the city that served as the capital from then on—now known as Tokyo. The Tokugawa government, the Bakufu, moved quickly to stamp out the dangerous foreign religion. It banned Christian missionaries, made martyrs of converts, and in 1639, closed Japan off from free contact with the rest of the world—a move that was to have an enormous effect on the nation's subsequent work. After a brief nine decades of interaction with Europeans, Japan became a world unto itself, a sleeping beauty dreaming its own identity, its face turned inward.

The prince whose rude kiss awoke the island country to international involvement was a rough-and-tumble adolescent of a nation, itself less than a hundred years old, the destiny of which would remain intertwined with Japan's thenceforth: the United States of America. In 1854 Commodore Matthew Calbraith Perry, with the persuasive aid of his warships' cannons, forced the Bakufu to sign a treaty of amity and friendship with the United States—The Treaty of Kanagawa—and open two ports, Hakodate and Shimoda, to foreign trade.

Deeming that treaty less than satisfactory, however, the United States sent a consul, Townsend Harris, to Japan to conclude a new commercial treaty. In August of 1856 Harris landed at the treaty port of Shimoda, located at the southern tip of the Izu Peninsula, to the south of the city of Edo. Nearly two years later, in June of 1858, Japan and the United States also signed a treaty of amity and commerce—The Treaty of Edo. Soon afterward Holland, Russia, England, and France each concluded nearly identical treaties. After nearly two-and-a-half centuries of isolation, Japan had rejoined the world. Our story begins the following year.

1

The
Instructions

R utherford Alcock was Britain's first consul general to Japan. Originally a surgeon, he had practiced in Amoy, one of the five treaty ports on the China coast. When an attack of rheumatic fever affected his hands, making it impossible for him to perform surgery, he had turned to diplomacy. Though not a lifelong career diplomat, he had been living in China for over ten years at the time he was called to Japan.

During those years, China had opened to the West in a limited way. After losing the Opium War to Britain, China was compelled to sign the Treaty of Nanking, thus making it, however reluctantly, open to intercourse with Europe. The Chinese, however, were ambivalent about this new openness. Those who wanted to let in the new light and those who wished to keep the old darkness continued to do battle.

The Chinese word for *China* means Middle Kingdom, indicating that China is the center around which other, subordinate nations revolve. Unshakable faith in their own superiority influenced the Chinese in their dealings with the Western barbarians, even after losing a war to England and being forced to open their ports. They flouted the treaty in ways calculated to incense the Europeans, who cherished beliefs of their own regarding race, culture, and the manifest destinies of empires.

Rutherford Alcock was a man of firm resolve. Faced with Chinese obstinacy and cunning, he countered by making the fulfillment of the treaty and respect for its spirit the keynote—

one might say fetish—of his diplomacy. That the Chinese had signed under coercion—with British guns pointed at their heads—did not alter his determination in the slightest; he would use any means necessary, economic sanctions or even military force, to make the Chinese adhere to the treaty. This, he believed, was his duty as Her Majesty's representative in China.

A widower who had lost his wife to illness several years earlier, Alcock had dark-circled eyes, sunken cheeks and a grayish pallor that betrayed a predisposition to gastric complaints. He was known to be irritable and given to fits of rage. He was also known to abhor compromise regarding his fetish, fulfillment of the treaty.

Alcock received official notice of his reassignment to Japan in the spring of 1859. Along with the announcement came a set of diplomatic instructions from the British government unlike any ever seen on the China coast. Alcock was to "win the confidence of the Japanese people" and "be content with gradual progress." The government, in short, had made a 180-degree turnabout from its ruthlessly aggressive policy toward China, in which Alcock had been a willing agent. It was now instructing him to take a gentler approach to treaty adherence in his new assignment. The treaty was to remain a priority, but Alcock was instructed to insist upon its fulfillment in patient manner, refrain from pressure, and take pains to avoid offending the Japanese government. And this new approach was not limited to Britain's instructions to Alcock.

According to the Treaty of Edo, the commercial treaty Japan had signed with Britain (it had also negotiated similar versions of the treaty with the United States, Holland, Russia, and France), three ports—Hakodate, Kanagawa, and Nagasaki—were scheduled to open on July 1, 1859.

Japan had been isolated during the Edo Period—but not totally. The Bakufu had allowed strictly limited trade with the Dutch and Chinese at Nagasaki, Japan's westernmost port and the closest to China. Then, in March 1854, the Japanese signed a treaty of amity and friendship with the United States (the Treaty of Kanagawa) and a similar agreement with Britain shortly thereafter. These pacts stated that if Japan agreed to any new treaties with other nations, the provisions would automatically be applied to the United States and England. Accordingly, when Japanese officials at Nagasaki concluded commercial treaties with Russia and Holland in October of 1857, permitting trade at Nagasaki and Hakodate, the United States and England were also beneficiaries. Merchant ships from both nations began visiting the two ports in 1858.

But they also brought in goods that, according to an official British government dispatch, "even if the treaty were ratified and trade duly opened, could not legally be imported into Japan." Determined to prohibit smuggling and other lawless acts that had marred the opening of ports in China, the British government issued a royal proclamation that British violators of Japanese law would be subject to applicable fines or other penalties and could expect no protection from Her Majesty's government. Commanders of British warships in Japanese ports and waters were ordered "to support by all lawful means the Tycoon [the titular head of the Bakufu, also known as the Shogun] of Japan and his government in preventing any violation, evasion or contravention by British subjects of the laws of Japan, or of the provisions of the said Treaty." Needless to say, Britain had never issued such a proclamation in relation to China.

The British government was demonstrating a friendly, some might say suspiciously friendly, attitude toward Japan—but why? As Alcock ruminated on the reasons for this new development, he smiled wryly to himself; it was all so obvious.

One reason was the need to contain the Russians, who had been advancing south from the Kamchatka Peninsula. But oddly enough, a moral consideration carried more weight—Britain was having a collective attack of Victorian guilt over its conduct in China.

A military-commercial superpower whose empire was unsurpassed in size and power, Britain had ruthlessly had its way in China, forcing the Chinese to accept an addictive commodity, opium, while reaping enormous profits as the sole supplier. When the Chinese resisted, the British had applied overwhelming military pressure in the form of the 1839 Opium War. Not satisfied with the concessions wrested from Chinese in this conflict—or the narrow interpretation of treaty rights by Chinese authorities—Britain, together with France, had gone to war again in 1856. This conflict, known as the Arrow War, or the Second Opium War, resulted in the signing of a new treaty with China—the Treaty of Tientsin—in June 1858.

The British government found itself in a quandary. The opium trade was universally agreed to be evil, but it also brought money pouring into the national coffers. Should Britain abandon it, how would it replace the enormous revenue that would be lost? Parliament and the public would not readily accept a large tax increase. Even so, they continued to loudly oppose the opium trade, and heap special abuse on the diplomats in China who oversaw it. Though he hated the trade himself, Alcock found such self-righteous hypocrisy infuriating.

The policy of establishing friendly relations with Japan was thus designed to appease an outraged home public and make amends for past misdeeds in Asia. It galled Alcock that he was being asked to behave as a helpless virgin before the Japanese—to approach them with hands meekly folded and head demurely bowed. He suspected that they would prove to be as wily and unscrupulous as the Chinese, their cultural forbears. Not to take a firm hand from the outset would encourage the Japanese to flout the treaty and form a contemptuous opinion of foreigners in general. There was no guarantee that they would fulfill the treaty and respect its spirit—the sacred tenets of his diplomacy. These instructions, Alcock thought, were indeed a bitter pill to swallow.

※

Alcock left his post at Canton for Japan on May 1, two months before the beginning of trade under the new treaties. It was already summer in that southern climate, and the burning rays of the summer sun glittered on the Pearl River as Alcock boarded the *Williamette*, a steamer that would take him to Hong Kong on the first leg of his journey.

Soon after leaving the landing of the Bogue forts, the *Williamette* passed a British ship with its flag at half-mast. Alcock was told that it carried the remains of an old adversary, Yeh Ming-ch'en, the former imperial commissioner at Canton.

"Farewell, Yeh, you godless old reprobate," he muttered under his breath. Watching the ship pass, Alcock reflected on the lessons he learned from the late commissioner about the Asian mentality.

For many years, European diplomats had tried to gain audience with the Chinese government, which, ensconced in its stronghold in Peking, saw no reason to acknowledge the disagreeable presence of these foreign devils—or welcome the change in the balance of power that they represented. They hoped that foreigners, like the demons they resembled, might go away if ignored.

But European diplomats were not so easily discouraged. Barred from establishing diplomatic missions in the capital, Peking, they took up residence in Canton and the other treaty ports. There they negotiated with imperial commissioners like Yeh, who were reluctant to make appointments with foreigners—and casually broke them. Also, despite a specific provision in the Treaty of Nanking, the Chinese forbade the Europeans from residing inside the city walls of Canton. How it galled the Europeans to be snubbed by these yellow-skinned pagans, whose faith in their own superiority rivaled their own!

The British decided to revenge these snubs by waging the Arrow War, which quickly settled the question of which side had superior military power. It took the combined Anglo-French forces but a day to topple the walls of Canton—and throw open its gates to European residence. The British captured Yeh in the siege of Canton and shipped him to Calcutta, where he died. The ship passing the *Williamette* was returning Yeh's remains to Chinese soil.

Alcock turned his gaze to the Bogue forts, now in ruins. They reminded him of a story he had heard about Yeh, one of many. Unlike France, the United States—then a young, struggling nation—had declined Britain's invitation to participate in the Arrow War, and had maintained a stance of neutrality. But because the United States had to protect its citizens living on the China coast, it had sent a sloop, the *Portsmouth*, to Canton. Arriving in Canton, the *Portsmouth* had lowered its boats. Boarding them, the ship's sailors had rowed toward the landing. Suddenly, the Chinese had started firing on them from the Bogue forts, which the *Williamette* was now passing. The sailors had desperately waved the Stars and Stripes, to no avail. The Chinese had continued firing and the sailors had fallen, dead and wounded.

The American commodore had protested, demanding an explanation. Yeh's smooth reply had been all form and no content—an example of that Chinese sophistry so maddeningly familiar to European diplomats. Exasperated, the commodore had turned his guns on the forts, silencing four batteries and routing 20,000 Chinese troops. This was the United States' only military action on the China coast; it never entered the Arrow War.

In the face of such military power, so persuasively displayed, Yeh had had no choice but finally to meet with the foreigners. After expressing his apologies, Yeh had coolly asked the commodore to "send the flag of his nation, that in the future the Chinese officers might know and be able to recognize it."

Fifty years of diplomacy in China, thought Alcock. And look where matters stand! How does one cope with a people as maddeningly obstinate and illogical as these, he asked himself. As he watched the ship bearing Yeh's remains pass out of sight he determined to apply in Japan what he had learned in China from Yeh and men like Yeh: the only logic they would respond to was the logic of the sword. But what to do about Her Majesty's instructions?

✳

The *Williamette* arrived in Hong Kong that same day. Alcock debarked and spent ten days in the Crown Colony, during which time British and French warships gathered in the harbor. One year had passed since the Arrow War, and the warships had been assembled to escort the British and French envoys to Peking, where they were to exchange ratified copies of the Treaty of Tientsin with Chinese officials.

But word arrived that the Chinese had repaired the Taku forts at the mouth of the Peiho River and, far from intending to honor their agreement, were resolved to risk war. The allied warships prepared for battle and sailed north. Alcock pondered this latest example of Chinese deceit. Were these people entirely lacking in morals? Or were they simply deficient in diplomatic common sense? If so, the British and French forces would soon pound it into them.

At Canton, Alcock boarded the HMS *Sampson*, the corvette that was to take him first to Shanghai, and then on to Japan. At Shanghai several warships stationed in Central China had also assembled. One was the *Mississippi*, an aging paddle wheeler. The *Mississippi* signaled the *Sampson* that the American minister to Japan was on board. The *Sampson* replied that one of its passengers was the British consul general to Japan.

The American minister, Townsend Harris, had recently been promoted from the rank of consul general and therefore outranked Alcock. As etiquette demanded that Alcock go to Harris, he quickly boarded the *Mississippi* to pay his respects.

Though ranking higher than Alcock, Harris had even less diplomatic experience than his British colleague. He had begun his life in Asia as a supercargo—a kind of humble seagoing merchant. With absolutely no support from his home government, this novice at diplomacy had miraculously done what Britain and other great powers had gone to war with China to do—he had negotiated a commercial treaty with Japan, without a single warship and at no cost to his country. This was unquestionably an astounding achievement. Suddenly he was the toast of the foreign community in China. The Americans especially couldn't praise him highly enough. Subsequent commercial treaties Japan signed with Holland, Russia, England, and France were all modeled on the Harris treaty.

The meeting between the two men began awkwardly, but after a toast to their mutual health, they settled down and began to talk seriously about the task before them. Harris, the senior in years and rank, with two years and eight months in Japan behind him, spoke first.

"There are currently two problems in Japan," he said. "One is the absence of good communications between Edo, the capital, and the United States."

In all the time Harris had been in Japan, his government had not given him even one ship-of-war. This was to be Alcock's fate as well. Soon after dropping him off in Japan, the HMS *Sampson* would turn around and head back to China. This was in line with the "instructions" regarding Britain's friendly intentions toward Japan, and the fact they had no commercial interests to protect there.

Harris took out a map of Japan and pushing aside the remains of their dinner, spread it out on the table. He outlined the various communications alternatives, limited though they were. "First of all," he said, "we have no choice but to rely on commercial sailing vessels to carry our communications both to China and back home. At the moment, these ships are only sailing from Nagasaki to Shanghai. Now that Kanagawa"—Harris indicated the new treaty port, thirty miles south of Edo—"is open, ships will soon be coming and going from there on a regular basis, but we can't count on having one ready at a moment's notice. And, depending on the weather, it takes from six to ten days to reach Shanghai from Kanagawa."

"What about overland communications?" asked Alcock.

"Well, one sure way is to use the Japanese government's system. But even that takes thirty days to send a message from Edo to Nagasaki. Sixty days round-trip. In fact, you can count on a letter taking seventy days to reach London, via Shanghai—which means that the round-trip from Edo to London and back requires two hundred days altogether. It's maddeningly slow."

Alcock pondered this daunting information. "You mentioned another problem," he said.

"Yes," continued Harris. "They're trying to isolate us in Yokohama, turn it into another Dejima." Alcock, who had read *Commodore Perry's Journal of an Expedition to Japan*, knew exactly what he meant. In that book Perry had described how, during the Edo Period, when Japan had carried on limited trade with the Dutch and Chinese, the Dutch in port had been strictly confined to a tiny man-made island in Nagasaki Harbor called Dejima, joined to the coast by a narrow bridge, thus preventing any mixing with the native population. Alcock, still angry when he recalled the ban against Europeans inside the city walls of Canton, strongly agreed with Harris that a similar situation must be prevented from developing this time.

"This is the crux of the matter," said Harris. "The Japanese are claiming that the open port specified in the treaty is not Kanagawa, a long-established post town on the Tokaido Road that runs from Edo to Kyoto, but Yokohama, a tiny fishing village located here," he said, indicating a point on the coast. "As you can see, Yokohama faces Kanagawa across the water, but the treacherous coastline makes communication by land between the two virtually impossible. The Japanese argue that the harbor at Yokohama is superior, which I admit is correct. But their true aim is to isolate us there from the rest of the country—to shut us up in another Dejima, as it were. That's why I oppose the designation of Yokohama as the open port."

Alcock saw now that the Japanese had no intention of fulfilling the treaty or respecting its spirit. Thinking of what lay ahead—and how his hands had been tied by his government's well-intentioned instructions—Alcock felt his hackles rising.

Alcock left Shanghai on May 31. The opening of the ports was scheduled for July 1, and he was eager to begin grappling with the many and various challenges he foresaw in his new position. First of all, he wanted to take a careful look at Nagasaki, where the British, Dutch, and other nationalities were already engaged in trade with the Japanese. And then, upon reaching Edo—the seat of the Tycoon's government—he intended to find suitable quarters there, unless the Japanese decided not to honor the stipulation in the treaty that permitted him to do so— a distinct possibility.

The voyage across the East China Sea took four days instead of the usual two, because of blinding rainstorms. The *Sampson* sailed into Nagasaki Harbor in the middle of a torrential down-pour. Undaunted, Alcock stood on the deck, peering through the slanted streaks of gray. As the ship entered the harbor from the south, he saw the city to his right and, directly ahead, a tiny island rising up from the water. "Dejima," he whispered to himself. So this was the ghetto the Japanese had built to contain the Dutch.

Alcock was astounded at the number of foreign ships anchored in the harbor. Good heavens, he remarked to himself, silently counting. He saw merchant ships flying English, French, Russian, and American flags, and a Russian man-of-war, fifteen foreign ships in all. They're here because of the prices, he thought.

One year earlier, news of astonishingly low prices in Japan—as little as a third of those in China—had reached Europeans living on the China coast. Only a short while before, Japanese prices had been notoriously high. One ton of medium-grade Nagasaki coal, for example, had jumped in price from four dollars to five, but was still one-third the cost of comparable coal in Shanghai. American warships, needing more coal than their depot in Shanghai could supply, frequently traveled to Nagasaki to supplement their stock. The Russians had not only made Nagasaki their primary source of coal in East Asia, but established a naval base there.

The European merchants in China were excited by the thought of the fortunes to be made in Japan, but also skeptical. From being the most expensive country in the world, Japan had suddenly become the cheapest. It seemed too good to be true. Nevertheless, they began sending merchant ships to Nagasaki soon after Japan signed commercial treaties with Holland and Russia in October 1857.

Arriving in Nagasaki laden with cotton goods, woolen goods, and sugar, they sought out Japanese goods, such as marine products, pottery, and silk, that they could sell back home. Silk was in particular demand: the spread of pebrine, a silkworm disease, had caused production in Europe to fall drastically, making low-priced Japanese silk very attractive.

In accordance with the supplemental treaties, a bazaar had been built in Nagasaki where Japanese and foreign merchants could meet and bargain with one another—the form of trade permitted by the treaties. But the foreign goods did not sell. Foreign traders, who had rented warehouses in anticipation of making a killing in this land of low prices, soon had to decide between two alternatives: leaving their goods in storage or shipping them back to China.

Currency exchange presented another problem. Fearful of British naval power, Nagasaki officials allowed the crews of warships to change all the money they required. But they had nothing but scorn for merchants and other foreign civilians— and showed it by permitting them to change only four dollars per person per day.

They raised the per-day exchange limit to ten dollars after a British man-of-war sailed menacingly into Nagasaki Harbor. But ten dollars a day, roughly equivalent to the monthly wage of a British or American seaman, was hardly sufficient for the foreign merchants, who had brought with them thousands of dollars with which to conduct trade.

While Alcock was still in Nagasaki, a group of British merchants led by William Keswick of Jardine, Matheson & Company, the largest British trading firm in the Far East, paid him a call on board the *Sampson*. Keswick outlined the grim situation vis-à-vis the Japanese authorities. "These are the latest barriers thrown up by the Japanese government, which has been extremely unfriendly toward commercial intercourse," he said, after enumerating the various problems.

Alcock nodded. The more he heard about the situation, the more clearly he realized that following his instructions to the letter would play directly into the hands of the Japanese: he would be leading his countrymen, like so many sheep, to the slaughter.

Keswick continued, saying, "The merchants in Nagasaki will not even accept notes issued by their own government at face value. Some refuse to take them at all. And they continue to refuse to take dollars, which they should do under the treaty."

The only alternative was barter, the form of trade most favored by the Japanese merchants.

"In that case, however, Japanese goods are not cheap at all. Moreover, Chinese guilds monopolize trade in marine products, and the Japanese authorities forbid us from taking part in it."

Like the Dutch, the Chinese were contained in their own ethnic ghetto in Nagasaki. But their trade guilds controlled all commerce in marine products, which prevented any participation by Europeans.

"From the chartering of sampans to the hiring of coolies— the authorities meddle in everything. One thing I'm sure of," added Keswick, "the Japanese government has its fingers in every pie. Nothing happens here without their noticing it."

Alcock nodded. This state of affairs was disappointing but not surprising. The Treaty of Edo had not yet taken effect— trade was then being conducted under the supplementary treaties with Holland and Russia, which only applied to the United States by extension. Alcock decided that this was neither the time nor the place to confront the authorities.

He spent two weeks in Nagasaki, during which time he was able to secure a promise from the local governor that, beginning July 1, he would implement reforms in response to the complaints of Keswick and other British merchants. The day before he left, the *Mississippi*, with Harris aboard, arrived in Nagasaki Harbor several days behind schedule.

✳

Not stopping at the treaty port of Kanagawa, the *Sampson* headed directly for Edo, but was forced to anchor off Shinagawa, a town on the Edo Bay, because of dangerous shoals off the coast.

Alcock was pleasantly surprised to find that the Japanese authorities did not object to his residing in Edo. He proceeded to search for a suitable site for the temporary British consulate and soon found one: the Buddhist temple of Tozenji in Tanakawa. Located near the Shinagawa coast, Tozenji would allow for a speedy escape by sea, should it ever prove necessary.

By then it was June 29. The ports mentioned in the Treaty of Edo—Hakodate, Kanagawa, and Nagasaki—were scheduled to open for the British in only two days, on July 1. In their version of the treaty, the Americans had designated July 4 for the opening of the ports, but the British, not wanting to associate this happy occasion with unpleasant memories, had chosen an earlier date.

In addition to Captain F. Howard Vyse, who was to become acting consul at Kanagawa, the British consulate staff included a first assistant who was studying Japanese, a Dutch interpreter, and two student interpreters, for a total of five. On July 1, Alcock and the five members of his party boarded the *Sampson* and together with nearly 200 pieces of baggage, headed for Kanagawa.

Keeping the shore to her right, the *Sampson* sailed toward the harbor. When she entered it, Alcock and the others could see Kanagawa on their right, Yokohama on their left.

Other than the now-familiar *Mississippi*, which was resting at anchor, Alcock and the others could see only one merchant-man. As the ship advanced into the harbor they could make out the features of Kanagawa and Yokohama. As the contours of the surrounding land gradually became clearer, Alcock and the others were transfixed by the sight of Yokohama.

When Alcock had met Harris in Shanghai, Harris had described Yokohama as a rustic little village. But the Yokohama before him was nothing of the sort.

Even from a distance it was possible to see that the houses lining the streets—and there were already a fair number of them—had been built recently. Some were still under construction. Lowering their gaze to the shoreline, Alcock and the others could see two piers jutting out into the water. The larger one looked big enough for twenty boats to land their passengers or cargoes at the same time.

I'd like to see them try it . . . , thought Alcock.

The Japanese government had evidently built these piers in the four months that Harris had been away from Japan. In other words, they had hurried to transform Yokohama into another

Dejima. It was clear that the Japanese had no intention of abiding by either the letter or the spirit of the treaty. It was also obvious to Alcock that the new barriers the Japanese had erected against European trade in Nagasaki represented yet another attempt to gut the treaties.

The *Sampson* stopped its engines and dropped anchor. Alcock had the crew quickly lower a boat. Boarding it, he and his party headed for the larger of the two piers. When the boat reached the end of it, Alcock got out. Made of granite, the pier had been built to a neck-craning height of nearly twelve feet, surmounted by a six-foot grass embankment. Alcock climbed the stone steps leading to the top and walked out onto it.

Looking out at the larger pier again, Alcock estimated that it was about a hundred yards long. Glancing toward Yokohama, he saw an official-looking building at the end of the pier. Alcock approached it. In front of the building was a black painted gate, before which sat several officials and an interpreter.

"What kind of building is this?" Alcock asked.

"It is the customshouse," an official answered.

At the invitation of the official, Alcock and his party entered the customshouse. Inside, he saw a neat sand-covered courtyard surrounded on all four sides by buildings. Some of the buildings were still under construction. Alcock had a distinct impression of haste.

Alcock was shown to a room. There he found five men, all clean-shaven, who were introduced as governors of foreign affairs. Later, he would drop this unwieldy appellation and simply call them by their Japanese title—*bugyo*. Soon, Alcock and the others were served Japanese sake and food that they did not find much to their taste.

"European diplomats in the East should present a united front, even if their home governments are quarreling. If they seem to be in disarray, Orientals will be quick to take advantage of them."

This was an iron rule of diplomacy in the East that all European diplomats understood. Alcock and Townsend Harris, his senior colleague on board the *Mississippi*, had to carefully plan their counterattack against the Japanese, who were trying to isolate foreigners in their preferred open port of Yokohama. Accordingly, Alcock did not discuss the problems of the foreign settlements and the open ports on this occasion.

Leaving the customshouse, Alcock and his party went to the Government Exchange Bank to change their money for Japanese currency before sallying forth into the Japanese commercial district.

At the Government Exchange Bank, they found two officials sitting very straight, their legs folded under them. Before them was a large box full of new gold and silver coins. Beside the box was a set of scales and leads.

Treaty articles related to currency—Article Five of the American and Article Ten of the British treaty—stated that foreign currency could be exchanged for its Japanese equivalent in weight and type. In other words, gold coins could be exchanged for gold coins and silver coins for silver coins of the same weight. The new silver and gold coins, as well as the scales and leads, were to be used for exchanging coins of similar type and weight, as stipulated in the treaties.

At this time, Europeans in East Asia did not generally carry gold coins. Instead, they used silver coins and Mexican dollars—principally the latter. Members of Alcock's party took out their dollar coins and handed them to the officials to exchange them for new Japanese silver coins. The official placed the dollars on one scale. On the other he placed twice the number of square silver coins. The scales balanced perfectly.

Alcock and his party had been told that the square silver coins were called ichibus (which they wrote as "itziboos" or "ichiboos"), and that one Mexican dollar weighed about as much as three ichibus.

However there were only twice as many silver coins on the scale as dollars. These new silver coins weighed one and a half times more than the old ichibus. In other words, one silver coin was worth one and a half ichibus. After changing their dollars for these new ichibus, Alcock and his party went out into the main street, which was opposite the front entrance of the customshouse.

Viewed from the sea, the customshouse was a little to the right of the center of Yokohama. The Japanese commercial district had been built to the right of the customshouse, in the town's northwest sector. To the left of the customshouse—the southeast sector—was empty land that was to be the site of the foreign settlement. Alcock and his party walked down the main street, toward the Japanese commercial district.

The store fronts displayed a wide selection of goods, including lacquerware, porcelain, pottery, fabrics, cabinetwork, and various types of handiwork. Some shopkeepers were setting out and arranging their stock. Goods that had just been delivered were lying about helter-skelter, still unpacked.

Wanting to browse, Alcock stopped in front of a shop selling Japanese sundries. A clerk showed him a glovebox and thrusting out six fingers, cried "six ichibus!"

One dollar was three ichibus. A younger member of Alcock's party decided he wanted the case and took two dollar coins from his pocket. The clerk looked at them and shook his head. As in Nagasaki, Japanese merchants would not accept dollars.

"All right. What about these?" asked the young Englishman, taking out the new coins that he had just received. One was worth one and a half ichibus, so four were worth six. The Englishman handed the clerk four coins. The clerk, however, was not satisfied—he thrust out four fingers twice. He wanted eight more of the new coins.

"Why, the extortionate Jew!" sputtered the Englishman. Watching this exchange, Alcock realized that something was fundamentally amiss. He asked his interpreter, Dan, to find out what the problem was. A Japanese castaway, Dan had been working on board the *Mississippi* as a stoker when he heard that the British consul in Canton had been appointed consul general to Japan. Thinking to return home as the world's first cosmopolitan Japanese, Dan had talked his way past the gates of the

Canton consulate and, becoming Alcock's interpreter and servant, accompanied him to Japan.

Dan looked at the Chinese characters that had been engraved on the front and reverse of the new silver coin. Nodding his head repeatedly, he listened to the clerk's explanation. Finally, his eyes grew wide with amazement. He turned to Alcock and the others.

"All right? Please don't be surprised." His eyes, however, were telling them to prepare for a shock.

"This silver coin is a freshly minted nishu."

What on earth was a nishu? Alcock's party asked Dan to explain.

"A nishu is worth only half as much as an ichibu."

"What . . . ?" they exclaimed in unison.

"I wonder whether this is really in accordance with the Japanese monetary system—or a simple swindle," mused Alcock. He pressed Dan to explain further.

"This new nishu weighs one and a half times more than the ichibu," Dan continued.

Alcock's party became increasingly agitated and demanded to know what was going on.

"Wait a moment," Alcock interjected. "Let's consider the facts here. In the Japanese monetary system, one nishu is worth only half an ichibu. But one nishu weighs half again as much as one ichibu. Why?"

Alcock's party fell silent, waiting for him to continue.

"When we change one dollar for nishu by weight, we receive two nishus. In effect, we are exchanging our dollar for one ichibu. But if we were to change our dollar for ichibus, we would receive three ichibus. Originally, one dollar could be changed for three ichibus, but now, with the introduction of the nishu, it is being changed for one. Now I understand—this is a means of beating down the value of the dollar to one-third."

Alcock's party was outraged:

"What a filthy snare!"

"An underhanded plot!"

"This is a scheme to make Japan, the cheapest country in the world, the most expensive!"

His party continued their chorus of complaints. Acting Consul Vyse said, "It amazes me that the Japanese would have prepared such a despicable means of violating the treaty so soon after the opening of the country."

"Indeed," replied Alcock, lapsing into silence.

To Alcock this was a greater blow than the attempt to transform Yokohama into another Dejima. The new barriers to trade that he had discovered in Nagasaki were nothing compared to this. This was more than just gutting and ignoring the treaties—it was a boldfaced challenge. It was as though the Japanese were tearing up the treaties, trampling on them, and issuing a declaration of war.

✳

Following this incident, Alcock went directly to the *Mississippi* to discuss with Harris the two problems that seemed most pressing: the transformation of Yokohama into another Dejima-style ghetto, and the issuing of the nishu.

He had already seen how Yokohama was being transformed. He had no doubt that the Japanese government intended to make Yokohama the open port mentioned in the treaties, build a foreign settlement there, and compel foreigners to live in it.

How should Britain, as a treaty signatory, respond? First, Alcock decided, he would establish the vice-consul in the original treaty port of Kanagawa, instead of Yokohama. Next, he would have the foreign merchants who had arrived aboard trading ships (he had seen but one so far) reside in Kanagawa instead of Yokohama as well. In short, he intended to thwart the Japanese government's scheme. Then, he would go to Edo and firmly demand that the Japanese government close Yokohama and make Kanagawa an open port. This, in general, was what he wanted to discuss with Harris.

The problem presented by the nishu, however, was different: it was not what it appeared on the surface. If his senior colleague knew anything about it, Alcock wanted to be briefed on everything, in detail. And it was imperative that he discuss this problem with Harris so that they could present a united front in the future.

Why had the Japanese government issued this currency? Harris felt that he knew the reason all too well. When Alcock asked him for an explanation, Harris quickly answered, "I had better start from the beginning, when Commodore Perry first visited Japan. Have you read his *Journal*, in which he describes what happened during his stay here?"

"Yes."

"It's all in there."

Perry had come to Japan twice. The first time was in July 1853. After delivering a letter from the President of the United States to the "emperor of Japan" (actually the Tycoon) urging the opening of the country, Perry had immediately departed for the China coast. His second visit was in February of the following year. This time, Perry dug in his heels; he was determined, at all costs, to obtain a treaty.

On his second visit, Perry came with a squadron of seven ships. Because their stay was prolonged, his ships required supplies of wood, water, food, and coal. Perry obtained these supplies from the Japanese, intending to pay for them as a matter of course. He had no desire to accept gifts from a country he was threatening with military force.

But how were the two sides to value their principal currencies—the round Mexican dollar and the square ichibu? What should the dollar be worth in ichibus? In short, they had to set an exchange rate. Perry had to negotiate this problem not only for his squadron but for all Americans who would come to Shimoda and Hakodate—the two ports opened by the Treaty of Kanagawa. Perry did not want to decide this matter carelessly. He instructed his two negotiators—pursers Speiden and Eldridge—that the exchange rate set was to be regarded as temporary, but that he wished to conduct thorough discussions to prepare for a formal decision in the future.

After signing the Treaty of Kanagawa at Yokohama, Perry

turned back toward Shimoda. There he began negotiating codicils to the treaty.

By weight, a Mexican dollar was worth three ichibus. Conversely, one ichibu was worth only one-third of a Mexican dollar.

The Japanese, however, insisted that one ichibu had the same value as one Mexican dollar, which weighed three times more. They argued that the exchange rate should be one ichibu to one dollar because the ichibu was engraved with the government stamp. Although this "stamp" consisted of nothing but Chinese characters engraved on the front and back of the coin, the Bakufu claimed that, by engraving its stamp, it had arbitrarily tripled the value of the coin. The Mexican dollar was only silver bullion, said the Japanese. It was not possible to compare it by weight with the ichibu.

This struck the negotiators as strange reasoning, to say the least. Whether the Mexican dollar and ichibu were considered "bullion" or "coins," they were both definitely silver. How was it possible to triple the value of the ichibu merely by engraving it with a government stamp?

Engraving this stamp did not require any complex skills or techniques. Anyone could make counterfeit coins and probably would, if enough money were to be made from it. The government would not be able to stop counterfeiting completely, no matter what punishments it imposed. In no time, they reasoned, counterfeit coins would flood the country and, in the end, the government would not be able to achieve its goals. With that thought in mind, the two pursers demanded an exchange rate of three ichibus to the dollar. That, they thought, was fair, since both coins were undoubtedly silver and one Mexican dollar weighed the same as three ichibus.

During the negotiations, which were held for three days at Ryozenji Temple in Shimoda, neither side would yield an inch. After the meeting on the third day, the two pursers made the following report to Perry: "Because the Japanese insist that the value of the ichibu is three times that of the dollar, they say they will pay us reckoning on a three-to-one basis. They seem to be making a bold attempt to cheat the United States Navy out of twice the amount of silver coins."

When he heard this news, Perry wanted to return to the United States as quickly as possible. The treaty signing had been completed: all that remained was the signing of the codicils. Their stay had stretched on to more than four months; both Perry and his crew had tired of Japan. Also, they had plenty of money. Not wanting to waste any more time, Perry compromised. While reserving a final decision for the future, he showed his magnanimity by agreeing to pay for ichibus at the rate the Japanese had requested and having done so, left Japan.

On returning to the United States, Perry made a report to the United States government concerning the currency question. The Japanese position as stated in the report drew loud protests from U.S. officials.

When they considered it carefully, U.S. officials realized that the Japanese position on the currency question was nothing but a makeshift excuse—the Japanese must have mistaken them for simpletons. It was a scheme to prevent the opening of the country.

Perry had opened Hakodate to serve as a port for the hundreds of whalers that prowled the North Pacific. Shimoda was to be the next coaling station after Hawaii on the regular sea route to China that would probably be opened in the future. But what would happen if the United States failed to counter the Japanese scheme?

The whaling ships calling at Hakodate and the packets loading on coal at Shimoda would have to pay triple the amount of silver for their water, wood, food, and coal. Consequently, no American ships would call at either port—exactly what the Japanese intended. If they were allowed to succeed in their scheme, the enormous expense and effort that the Perry expedition had entailed would all be for naught. Japan would remain in utter isolation.

Everyone who saw the report agreed: the Japanese must have mustered all their cunning to come up with this plan.

The U.S. government could not ignore the challenge

thrown down by the Japanese. If it did, the treaty with Japan would become meaningless, and worse, the prestige of the young nation itself would suffer. Somehow they would have to make the Japanese conform to the treaty through proper, serious negotiations.

Article Eleven of the Perry treaty provided for a consul and stipulated that this consul could be stationed at Shimoda. Based on this article, Townsend Harris was appointed consul general to Japan. In addition to concluding a commercial treaty, his responsibilities included resolving the currency problem. Harris had applied himself to these tasks with great energy.

Harris had been told to make the currency question his first order of business. He and Alcock were talking in the officers' mess aboard the *Mississippi*. It was now noon. When their food was brought in, Harris suddenly stopping speaking and urged Alcock to eat. While they were dining, Harris continued where he had left off.

"When I arrived at Shimoda, I immediately moved to resolve the currency problem. I felt that it was an important issue that had to be dealt with quickly. One reason was that I myself have been compelled to pay triple the price of goods here. It's absurd."

"Indeed it is," said Alcock emphatically.

"Commodore Perry and his men were not the only ones to pay triple prices. Merchantmen and warships who later visited Japan all had to pay at the same rate. The Japanese compelled them to use silver coins purchased at three times their true worth. The rumor spread among Europeans on the China coast that Japan had the highest prices in the world. Because of Shimoda's terrible reputation, I have had hardly any visitors. Ever since the visit of Commodore Perry, the Japanese government has continued its underhanded policy aimed at tripling prices for foreigners and effectively preventing anyone from coming to Japan. So far, that policy has succeeded brilliantly."

"I see."

"About one month after arriving at Shimoda, I discussed the currency question with the two Shimoda governors. The

governors gave me the same cock-and-bull story they had Commodore Perry, that the ichibu has the same value as the Mexican
dollar, which is three times its weight. I told them that what they
were saying was absurd and asked them what was unfair about
exchanging currency weight-for-weight. I very patiently explained that if they did not regard that as right and proper,
then truth and justice could not exist in this world."

"What happened then?"

"We discussed currency only that one time, but four months
later, the Japanese government quite coolly—yes, 'coolly' is the
most fitting word—withdrew all of their old demands. In short,
they finally admitted their error. You never know when the
Japanese will go back on their word."

"You are saying they are not people to be trusted."

"Precisely. That is why, just to be safe, I incorporated a
provision for the exchange of currency of the same type and
weight in Article Three of the Convention of Shimoda that I
concluded with the Shimoda governors, even though it was a
convention that did not require ratification. However . . ."

"Yes?"

"After signing the Convention of Shimoda, but before negotiating the Treaty of Edo, the Japanese concluded supplementary treaties with the Dutch and Russians at Nagasaki in which
they cleverly inserted an exchange rate of one ichibu to the
dollar. Furthermore, that exchange is of Japanese paper money
for our currency. You probably saw this in Nagasaki."

"Yes, I did."

"Those flimsy paper notes that they exchange . . . you know
what I mean. They try to get around exchanging currency
weight-for-weight by using paper money. They proposed an
exchange rate of one ichibu to the dollar with that aim in mind."

"How were they allowed to incorporate this scheme in the
Dutch and Russian treaties?"

"The main negotiator for the Treaty of Edo was Iwase, the
Prince of Higo, who had just signed the supplementary treaties
in Nagasaki. He has since been demoted and is no longer serving
in an important post. He was a very canny negotiator and a very

troublesome one for me. He insisted that the currency article be based on the supplementary treaties. Of course, I refused. When I turned him down firmly, he suddenly conceded and agreed to insert Article Five, which provided for the exchange of currency of the same weight and type, just as I had insisted. This provision was also included in the treaties with Holland, Russia, England, and France."

"Of course."

"The treaties clearly provide for the exchange of currency of equal weight and type. I was sure that they could no longer try their old, underhanded trick of charging foreigners triple the actual prices. But now they have made these silver coins called nishus that inflate the amount of silver three times. When the dollar and nishu are exchanged by weight, the dollar is devalued to one ichibu. This is nothing but a return to their old position. Their aim is to triple prices for foreigners. There is no end to the cunning of these Japanese," said Harris with a sigh.

"I am utterly amazed, Mr. Harris."

The situation was far worse than he had feared.

Alone in his quarters after his first day out in the Japanese marketplace, Alcock sipped his habitual beverage before retiring—a tepid infusion of comfrey and cloves for his agitated digestive system.

In his first days in his new post, it had became apparent to Alcock that two problems were of the utmost urgency: first, the Japanese seemed bent on isolating the foreign community in the port town of Yokohama, which had so hastily been converted from a sleepy fishing hamlet to a trading port with all the necessary facilities.

It was obvious to Alcock that the Japanese wished to change the treaty port from the original Kanagawa, a major post town with a long history and a thriving Japanese community, to Yokohama, where few Japanese would be "contaminated" by contact with Europeans. It galled him to be treated like a member of an unclean caste, and he determined they would not get away with it. Besides, he told himself: a treaty is a treaty, a man's word is his word. If nothing else, he most definitely intended to show the Japanese what an honorable agreement with England entailed.

The second problem was economic. Alcock's feverish, overactive mind was far from winding down for a night's repose as he put out the light and sat down on the bed. He reviewed the day's events in light of what he knew so far. The Japanese repeatedly insisted that their silver coin, the ichibu, bore a three-to-one relation to the Mexican silver dollar. They insisted that in spite of the indisputable one-for-one weight equivalence of the two, the ichibu should be valued at three times its weight in silver simply because they said so. The Bakufu's government stamp on the coin was the only justification they could give for their ridiculous claim. Surely they weren't so naïve as to think that that stamp could not be counterfeited by anyone with a talent for metalwork? And the new coin, the nishu, was just an indirect way of attaining the same end. And yet their position was inconsistent—sometimes agreeing to a weight-for-weight exchange, sometimes not.

Do they truly expect us to fall for such childish tricks, he wondered, silently renewing his commitment to the treaty as he fell into a fitful sleep.

In the dead of night his Japanese manservant in the next room awoke to the sound of agitated cries in the odd-sounding foreign tongue. "Not this time, Yeh!" called Alcock, tossing restlessly, "Not this time . . ."

2

Low Cunning

T he Bakufu had scheduled various diplomatic functions for Alcock. The first was a formal call on the minister of foreign affairs. Next was a ceremony to exchange the instruments of ratification. Afterward, the Japanese paid a call on the British mission to present gifts in return for the *Emperor*, a steam yacht that had been given to the Tycoon by the British queen. Although the gifts included a suit of armor and craftwork, the actual objects were not presented. Instead, Alcock was given a list of the gifts in a ceremony that struck him as wonderfully strange.

As planned, soon after the instruments of ratification were exchanged, the *Sampson* left Edo, carrying the British copies of the ratified Treaty of Edo. This hasty departure further irritated Alcock's already sensitive nerves.

Having heard from Harris in Shanghai about the poor communications between Shanghai and Kanagawa, Alcock sought an interview with the commander in chief of the China station, at which he requested the assignment of a man-of-war or gunboat—or if that was impossible, a communications vessel. The commander in chief, however, refused, saying that the squadron was in the process of being relieved and that nearly all his ships had been sent back to England. Given the unsettled situation in North China, he had no warships to spare.

And that indeed was the case: when the combined Anglo-French squadron assembled and headed north to exchange

ratifications, Central China and South China were left unde-
fended. Moreover, the situation in North China was truly
alarming.

Although Alcock did not know it, the combined Anglo-
French squadron had already suffered a major blow. While on
its way to exchange ratifications, the squadron had been fired
upon from the Taku forts at the mouth of the Peiho River. Four
gunboats had been sunk and several hundred men killed or
wounded.

Alcock understood the reason for the commander in chief's
refusal. He was well aware that warships were not regularly
stationed at all British legations and consulates. It would have
been an impossible task even for the British Navy, the greatest in
the world.

Even so, Alcock could not help feeling abandoned. He later
wrote:

> I never knew an Admiral, or a senior officer, I think,
> who did not seem to consider the first duty of the Com-
> mander of a ship of war, after dropping a Minister or a
> Consul in the midst of a semi-civilized population,—as a
> man drops an awkward burden,—was to disappear as fast
> as possible, and leave him to his destiny or his resources. . . .
> There is much to regret, and something I think to amend,
> in the practice of dropping diplomatic or consular agents
> in the most remote regions, and leaving them to take care
> of themselves as best they can, or to be sacrificed in the
> attempt,—before it can possibly be known either what are
> the conditions under which the duties are to be carried on,
> or the dangers and difficulties to be encountered.

Alcock made no attempt to hide his annoyance. He had not
yet overcome his feelings of abandonment when, on July 16, he
received a letter from the Japanese minister of foreign affairs. It
was in reply to a letter of protest that Alcock—then still off the
coast of Kanagawa—had sent the minister concerning the currency question.

The only foreign languages that the Japanese knew were

Dutch and Chinese. Ever since Perry's visit, Europeans had conducted their written and verbal communications with the Japanese in Dutch. Both sides always appended a Dutch translation to every document. A Dutch translation had also come with the minister's reply. Alcock's translator soon rendered it into English.

Alcock read through it quickly. The first part was a confusing mass of figures. Then came this paragraph: "Japanese silver coins have been repeatedly reminted and each time the amount of silver per coin has been decreased. Consequently, they have become a currency that does not have material value."

After this, the going suddenly became much easier:

> Japan has adopted the gold standard. Silver coins engraved with the government stamp are substitute currency for gold coins. They are thus like paper or leather bills and are good only in Japan. With the recent opening of the country, currency has come to be exchanged weight-for-weight. But because Japanese silver coins are the kind of substitute currency described above, they cannot be compared weight-for-weight with foreign silver coins. It would be like putting paper money on a scale and weighing it against silver coins. Therefore, we have measured the weight and purity of the dollar and minted comparable silver coins. We hope that you will understand our reasons for doing so. If you have any questions, please do not hesitate to ask.

The letter was nothing but a mass of Chinese-style sophistry.

One point bothered him in particular. The letter sweepingly stated that Japan had adopted the gold standard. But Harris had never told Alcock that the Japanese had made such a claim. Had Harris heard this previously? Or was this the first time? And, if it was the first time, what was their aim? The only way to clear up such doubts—or any other problem that might arise—was to consult Harris. Alcock mounted his horse and went to call on the American legation.

Harris had established his legation at Zenpukuji Temple in Azabu, about a thirty-minute walk from the British consulate general in Edo. The path from the gate of Zenpukuji to the main temple was lined on both sides with houses. Harris had rented the large house on the right as one approached the main temple. That was where Alcock found him.

"There's no end to the low cunning of the Japanese," said Harris. You are so right, thought Alcock.

"Once again they come forth with these ridiculous excuses," said Harris, scowling as he glanced through the letter. "What do you think, Mr. Alcock? The people and the government deliberately bestow excessive value on their gold and silver coins, asking for triple their worth. Do they really think they can get away with it? What kind of fools do they take us for?"

"They seem to be perfectly serious."

"But if we let them go through with their scheme, the country will immediately be flooded with counterfeit coins. Anyone can make ichibus and triple their money. So, in the end, they will not be able to achieve their aim. They will not be able to stop the counterfeiting, no matter how harshly they punish the offenders. Don't you agree? Consider this: no nation—however despotic or absolute its government—has ever successfully attempted such a thing in the history of the world."

Alcock had already considered this point. He had never read or heard of such a thing before. Harris eagerly continued, saying, "The Japanese government is trying to trick us by claiming to do the impossible. They are as shameless as thieves. This scheme of theirs is insolent, outrageous. In any event, I refuse to listen to their prattle about the gold standard and all the rest of it. Article Five of our treaty and Article Ten of yours both state that foreign currency shall be exchanged for the same type and same weight of Japanese currency. The articles also stipulate that, because the Japanese are not yet acquainted with foreign coin, Japanese customs officials will, for a period of one year after the opening of each harbor, furnish Americans with Japanese coin in exchange for ours, equal weights being given. It's all there in black and white. When we signed the treaty, one dollar was being changed for three ichibus. That's the way it should be."

When Alcock returned to the British consulate general that day, he had determined to answer the Japanese government.

> Giving reasons that are less than convincing, the Japanese government has tried to reduce the value of foreign currency to one-third. If we accept those reasons, the Japanese government will be able to lower the value of foreign currency as much as it likes—to one-tenth or one-twentieth its original value. There is no greater obstacle to trade than such a policy. But because our mission has various expenses to pay, rather than make further fruitless complaints, I am requesting that you send me two thousand ichibus, the silver coins that were still accepted when the treaty was signed with Japan.

Soon after, on July 21, Alcock received a notice announcing the abolishment of the nishu and the beginning of the exchange of equal weights and equal types of currency, on the condition that these measures be in force only "until negotiations can be arranged." Together with the notice, Alcock also received the 2,000 ichibus he had requested.

That afternoon, Harris paid Alcock a visit. "How are you getting along?" he asked. When Alcock told him the news, Harris did not look surprised.

"I see. So you have also had some ichibus delivered. You see how easily the Japanese go back on their word. They would as soon lie as breathe. This is also the Chinese government's usual method of conducting diplomatic relations, one you must have often encountered in China. You can see the same attitude in the Japanese government's handling of the currency question— there is absolutely no difference. In short, Mr. Alcock, we should ignore them. Yes, ignoring them is the best policy."

Alcock gave Harris his wholehearted assent.

Complaints were arriving in a steady stream from the foreign merchants in Yokohama.

They had come to the port loaded with goods. But, as in Nagasaki, they had been unable to sell any of them. Because paper money was not issued in Yokohama, they did not have to deal with the problem of Japanese merchants not accepting notes for the amount shown or refusing to take notes altogether. On the other hand, the nishu—the notorious nishu—had been circulated in Yokohama and, consequently, none of the foreign merchants could buy Japanese goods. The dollar fared no better: Japanese merchants in Yokohama refused to accept it. Bartering was the only alternative, but as in Nagasaki, that removed the advantages of trading in Japan.

✳

On July 20, nine merchant ships appeared in Yokohama harbor. The captain of one soon lost patience and left, leaving eight.

Nearly all of the foreign merchants had chartered ships. Every extra day they stayed meant a higher charter fee. It had been twenty days since the opening of the ports, and the demurrage had become hard for the merchants to bear. They had money for purchasing goods but none to spare. Also, they had to pay a high annual interest—about thirty-five percent.

Foreign merchants urged their vice-consuls to demand that the Japanese government not only remove currency barriers but also compensate them for losses from delays caused by those barriers.

Vice-consuls had been dispatched by three countries: the United States, Great Britain, and Holland. To thwart the Bakufu's attempt to isolate them in Yokohama, these countries had insisted on establishing their consulates in Kanagawa. Their vice-consuls bore the brunt of the merchants' complaints.

On July 22, the day after the ichibus had been delivered to Alcock and Harris in Edo, the Bakufu announced that it would allow foreign merchants in Yokohama an exchange rate of three ichibus to the dollar.

Soon after this announcement, however, something strange occurred.

The international ratio of gold to silver was one to sixteen.

In other words, one gram of gold was worth sixteen grams of silver throughout most of the world. In Japan, however, the ratio of the gold cobang to the silver ichibu was about one to five. That is, one gram of gold was worth about five grams of silver. But what did this discrepancy mean?

It meant, for example, that a merchant with one gram of gold could exchange it in Shanghai for sixteen grams of silver. He could then come to Yokohama with that sixteen grams and exchange it for three grams of gold. In short, he could triple his money. He could then return to Shanghai, exchange his gold for silver, bring the silver back to Yokohama . . . and so on.

By repeating this process again and again he could increase his earnings endlessly. That was what the discrepancy meant.

The foreign merchants were quick to discover this perpetual money-making machine.

On July 22, foreign merchants could obtain ichibus at the rate of three to the dollar. Of course, some used these ichibus to buy goods. But the first thing most merchants did with their new ichibus was buy the golden "merchandise" known as "kobans," or as the British called them, "cobangs." The merchants flocked to the Japanese commercial district and fought to get their hands on ichibus.

No words were needed for this kind of trade—ten fingers would do.

The standard unit of the Japanese monetary system was four. Thus, one cobang was worth four ichibus.

A foreign merchant thrusts four fingers at his Japanese counterpart. The Japanese, however, does not nod yes: he wants a premium.

The foreigner shows five fingers. Even then, the Japanese shakes his head no. The foreigner extends one finger of his other hand. "How about six ichibus?" he asks. The Japanese finally nods his head yes. At the rate of one cobang to six ichibus the Japanese can still make a profit of two ichibu—or fifty percent. The foreigner, however, can make even more. By taking his cobangs and selling them abroad he doubles his money. Cobangs were not bulky. Wrapped in small parcels, they could easily be transported to the China coast and sold. The proviso to the currency article stated that, except for copper coins, it was permissible to export Japanese currency. Because merchants were free to import and export, no one was so foolish as to make a customs declaration. Also, there were no customs duties. It was the easiest way imaginable of making a killing. Everyone began to join in the feverish rush for cobangs.

✳

Alcock soon heard about the growing cobang fever among the merchants from Acting Consul Vyse in Kanagawa.

Alcock had recently managed to obtain some ichibus himself. He had yet to see the gold coin called the cobang, however. The ratio of the gold cobang to the silver ichibu was one to five, extremely low compared with the parity of gold and silver in the rest of world. Thus foreign merchants were frantically searching for cobangs.

But a doubt arose in Alcock's mind. His senior colleague had been in Japan for a long time. He must have known about this low ratio. He must have foreseen this wild rush for cobangs and could have had the Japanese government take measures to prevent it. Alcock left immediately for the American legation to ask Harris for an explanation.

✳

When he met Harris, Alcock immediately posed the question that had been bothering him, though he knew he was being rudely direct.

"Didn't you know that the parity of gold to silver in Japan was one to five?"

"Yes, I knew," said Harris. "As you are no doubt aware, China has adopted the silver standard."

China was on the silver standard, but it had no silver coins. Instead, it used silver bullion as currency.

"Because it is on the silver standard, gold and gold coins cannot be used in trade. I thought that Japan was the same as

China. Japan is also on the silver standard, but it has a gold coin called the cobang, which is a kind of commemorative coin, like an American twenty-dollar gold piece. I have been to any number of shops in Shimoda, Edo, and Nagasaki, but I have yet to see it. Did you notice it when you were in Nagasaki?"

"No, I didn't."

Alcock had visited many shops in Nagasaki, but now that he thought of it, he had never seen any cobangs.

"But now that a fifty percent premium is being given for ichibus, cobangs have come tumbling out of the walls. It was careless of me not to notice. . . . But even though cobangs are not in common circulation, it is essential to know their purity. I recently sent cobangs and ichibus provided by the Japanese government to the Philadelphia mint for an assay."

While in Shanghai Harris had sent cobangs and ichibus to the United States to be tested for purity.

"They should be sending me the exact figures before long, but I already received a rough estimate in Shanghai. Would you mind waiting a moment?"

Harris went into a back room and came back with a sheet of paper.

"The Japanese gold cobang weighs about 11.3 grams," he said. "The gold content is around fifty-five percent. The remaining forty-five percent is silver. Therefore, one cobang is worth about four Mexican dollars, as measured by the international ratio of gold to silver. But in the Japanese monetary system, one cobang is worth four ichibus. That's the secret of how these merchants are doubling or tripling their money. It will be easier to understand if I illustrate it for you."

Drawing a diagram on a sheet of paper, Harris explained: "One dollar is worth three ichibus, so four dollars are worth twelve ichibus. They are here, on the left. But in the Japanese monetary system, one cobang is worth four ichibus. Therefore, twelve ichibus are worth three cobangs. As I mentioned before, one cobang is worth four dollars, according to the international ratio of gold to silver. Three cobangs are thus worth twelve dollars. They are here, on the right. In short, by changing

dollars for ichibus and ichibus for cobangs and changing cobangs for dollars, you can triple your money. This, then, is the
basic reasoning behind the gold rush in Yokohama. I must admit
I was astonished to find that there were so many cobangs in
Japan."

Alcock was still not completely satisfied. There was still one
more thing he wanted to know—"Have you informed the Japanese about this?"

"I had intended to inform them right away, but when I
arrived I found that nefarious coin, the nishu, waiting for me. I
was completely occupied with that. Also, the Japanese do not
ordinarily use coins, so I thought that there was no need to
hurry . . ."

Once again, Alcock was puzzled by Harris's answer.

"But why didn't you tell me?"

"Because of the circumstances I just mentioned."

But Harris hadn't appeared to be overly occupied with the
nishu problem. Also, he could have discussed this important
matter with Alcock in Shanghai or later, in Yokohama. In fact,
he had had a duty to tell him. Alcock was not satisfied with this
explanation.

"So that's the way things stand," said Harris. "You must tell
the Japanese that they can stop the flow of cobangs out of the
country by bringing the official rate of one cobang to four
ichibus into conformity with the international parity of gold and
silver. I will also inform them myself."

Walking back from the American legation, Alcock gradually
began to understand what hadn't been clear before about Harris's rather unconvincing explanation.

It had taken foreign merchants in Yokohama only twenty
days to realize that they could profit by buying cobangs and to
start a frantic hunt for them, paying a premium of fifty percent.

His senior colleague, however, had been in Japan for three
years. No matter how little the Japanese used cobangs, it was
unlikely that Harris would not have known what the foreign
merchants had discovered right away. And if he had noticed—
which was highly likely—he should have advised the Japanese to
take measures to prevent a wild rush for cobangs.

But Harris had done nothing. Why? Had he neglected his duty out of sheer carelessness? Somehow Alcock could not believe it.

The most likely explanation was that his senior colleague had joined the rush for cobangs himself. If he were to tell the Japanese that their ratio of gold to silver was unusually low and that they should adjust it, his cobang profiteering would come to an abrupt halt. Therefore he had not told them. No, thought Alcock, there could be no doubt about it.

$$*$$

There was, however, one more mystery that Alcock could not explain: the difference between currency prices in Japan and China.

When they learned about the rush for cobangs in Yokohama, the Japanese government asked Alcock about the relative values of money in China and other countries.

In Japan, one ichibu was worth 1,600 cash—the cash being an iron or copper coin that was the smallest unit of currency in China and Japan. Because one dollar was worth three ichibus, it was equivalent to 4,800 cash.

In China, however, silver was used to pay for opium and was thus constantly flowing out of the country. This caused the value of silver to rise steadily and that of cash to fall, making cash cheap. Even so, one dollar was valued at only 1,000 or 1,200 cash. But in Japan one dollar was worth 4,800 cash.

Why was it possible for the dollar to be worth so much? Alcock could not understand. He had no reply to the Bakufu's questions.

On July 31, exactly one month after the opening of the ports, Alcock received another letter from the Japanese government concerning currency.

After having it translated, Alcock read it: "Japan has many kinds of gold and silver coins with various indicated values and degrees of purity. But because they are engraved and circulated with the government stamp, there are no particular barriers to their use."

That was how it started. Still the same old verbal shell game. As Alcock was about to toss the letter away in irritation, he reminded himself that it was a diplomatic document. He couldn't very well lay it aside without reading it through. Restraining his displeasure, he pressed on:

> Twenty years ago the ichibu was reminted and its volume of silver reduced. It was then circulated only in Japan. It is not possible to use this kind of coin in trade. Consequently, we have increased its silver content and returned it to the form it had twenty years ago. This coin is the nishu. Coins that are engraved and circulated with the government stamp are like paper or leather bills. It is not possible to exchange these types of coins with foreign coins weight-for-weight. In weight-for-weight exchange, the coins themselves must have intrinsic value. If you agree that this is so, why then do you object to our recent action?

Alcock understood what they were trying to say. Their argument, of course, was entirely specious. But he also remembered that his senior colleague had said:

"If they issue this currency, the country will be immediately flooded with counterfeit coins and, in the end, they will not be able to achieve their aim. They will not be able to completely stop the counterfeiting, not matter how harshly they punish the offenders. There has never been a nation—however despotic or absolute the government—that has ever successfully attempted such a thing in the history of the world."

Harris was absolutely correct. The Japanese explanation could only be a pretext.

Once again, Alcock felt like throwing the letter away, but checked himself. He continued reading: "In terms of gold content, one twenty-dollar gold piece is worth five Japanese cobangs. Therefore, one cobang is worth four dollars."

Although Alcock doubted whether the Japanese had the technology to measure the purity of coins, their conclusion was correct. His senior colleague had said that while in Shanghai, he had confirmed that the cobang was worth four dollars.

The next paragraph, however, was clearly absurd. Its logic was nothing but a tissue of Oriental sophistry and cunning.

"In the Japanese monetary system, one cobang is worth four ichibus. One ichibu is thus equivalent to one dollar. Even if the ichibu were to weigh only one-third as much, it would still have the same value as one dollar."

Alcock's blood began to boil. Despite his exasperation, he continued:

"If the dollar and ichibu are exchanged weight-for-weight, all Japanese goods can be bought for one-third their true price, and the Japanese will have to pay triple the price for foreign goods."

Harris had told him that since Commodore Perry's visit, "tripling prices for foreigners and discouraging them from coming to Japan have become the Japanese government's standard, temporizing measures for resisting the opening of the country."

Although the letter seemed to be saying exactly the opposite, Alcock decided that it was just another example of their thievish audacity.

But where did the problem lie? After finishing the letter, Alcock turned it over carefully in his mind.

It all finally narrowed down to the low ratio of gold to silver: that was the problem. Just as Harris had said, the Japanese should adopt the international ratio of sixteen to one. That would solve everything. It would also end cobang profiteering.

But he felt it was up to Harris, who had already crossed swords with the Japanese over the currency question, to propose this solution to them.

Alcock's feeling that Harris had been buying cobangs was more a certainty than a suspicion. Also, Harris's comment that he had obtained a rough estimate of the cobang's purity in Shanghai suddenly stirred a new doubt in Alcock's mind. What had Harris been doing in Shanghai? He could have had this estimate made while he was there to exchange the cobangs he had brought from Japan.

Alcock was not totally convinced of this point, but he felt that, in any event, he should entrust this one problem to Harris. When he met Harris again, Alcock strongly urged him to advise the Japanese on the currency question.

He also sent a reply to the Bakufu, saying that he had no intention of discussing anything concerning gold.

Alcock was unable to explain the substantial difference between the price of cash in Japan and China; in his reply of August 9, he decided to ignore it.

The letter that had been sent to Alcock was also sent to Harris.

As far as Harris was concerned, the currency question had been settled. As long as the Japanese observed the weight-for-weight exchange provision in the treaty, he was satisfied.

But he did have to respond to two points in the Bakufu's letter.

One concerned the difference between the value of cash in China and Japan. This was something that Harris, like Alcock, could not understand. Harris wrote: "Iron is never used as money in civilized nations. Copper is used as money, but only in coins that have a lower value than silver coins." It so happened Japan used iron coins that had the same value as its copper coins.

The second point concerned measures for ending cobang profiteering. Alcock had prodded Harris to advise the Japanese government on this matter.

Harris offered the following advice: "The world ratio of gold to silver is one to sixteen. In Japan the ratio is one to five. This difference has led to the speculative buying of cobangs. I therefore urge you to issue a new cobang with a value one-third that of the present one and to make this new cobang equivalent to four ichibus. In other words, three of the new cobangs should be worth one of the present ones. If this is done, speculative buying of cobangs will cease."

A reply arrived from the Japanese. As always, Harris showed

the English translation to Alcock. "Here it is," he said wearily. Alcock did not want to look at it but, thinking that he may as well have a glance, began to read:

> To increase the number of its silver coins, Japan has decreased the amount of silver in each coin, engraved them with the government stamp as proof of their worth, and given them the same value as when they contained the full amount of silver. These coins are the ichibu. We have used the silver saved by decreasing the amount of silver in the ichibu to mint the nishu, in which the amount of silver has been increased. We have thus returned to the old monetary system. This, we believe, is a perfectly correct method.

This was nothing but another repetition of the old specious claim that the nishu was a sound currency.

The letter also argued that making three new cobangs worth onc present one, which Harris had suggested, and minting nishu were essentially the same. It offered the following reason for not accepting Harris's suggestion: "Japan is a gold standard country and the gold cobang is its key currency. If we triple the value of the cobang, prices would also triple. Therefore, we cannot increase the price of gold."

Gold was gold and silver was silver. It was totally impossible for gold to become the key currency of silver and for silver to become the auxiliary coin of gold. Alcock finished reading and looked up.

"How do you like it?" asked Harris. "The low cunning of the Japanese flows forth like a gushing spring—there is no end to it."

Alcock nodded in silent agreement, his stomach churning.

Alcock left his meeting with Harris in a quandary. Because Harris was his senior in age, rank, and experience in Japan, Alcock had naturally deferred to his assessments of the currency question and other matters. But now he had begun to suspect the man's motives. When Alcock learned that the cobang, Japan's gold currency, was valued in Japan at a five-to-one ratio to silver, whereas the international ratio was sixteen to one, Alcock asked himself again how long Harris had known this and why he had failed to inform the Japanese of their error. After all, it was part of his duty as a diplomat to inform and instruct, where need be. Harris's thin excuses simply did not hold water. To inform the Japanese would be to reduce the profits to be made in cobang speculation by a third. Harris could only be—shamefully—profiteering in cobangs himself, greedily draining the gold stores of a nation to which he was pledged in friendship, or at least to mutual, as opposed to one-sided, advantage.

Still, I haven't any proof, he said to himself as he returned home for the evening. Surrounded by wolves, he thought, and not a ship in port of our own. And yet Harris was the most knowledgeable ally Alcock had. He depended on Harris, and they must present a united front.

The exchange of explanatory letters among Alcock, Harris, and the Bakufu's administrators ended by settling nothing. The Japanese merely reiterated their position. Harris was right about one thing, Alcock thought grimly. The Japanese position was nothing but another example of Oriental guile.

3

The
Gold Rush

AUGUST–NOVEMBER, 1859

Alarmed by the rush on cobangs by foreign merchants, the Yokohama Government Exchange House stopped changing ichibus after only ten days. The date was August 1, exactly one month after the opening of the ports.

An exception, however, was made for ships' officers and crews, which allowed them to change fifty dollars a month per ship so that they could purchase everyday necessities.

A total of twelve merchantmen had entered the port of Yokohama. Three had left, leaving nine. Each of these nine ships was thus permitted to change fifty dollars a month.

The same chain of events—the withdrawal of the nishu, the decision to allow free exchange of the ichibu, and the sudden imposition of exchange limits—also occurred in Nagasaki.

Outraged by the Japanese government's action, the foreign merchants again complained to their vice-consuls. The vice-consuls also found the situation unacceptable; they began to register daily protests with Bakufu officials. Surprisingly, the Japanese government quickly caved in. On August 10, it announced that it would "exchange currency according to the circumstances."

Initially, the amount the Bakufu would change "according to the circumstances" was only one or two dollars per person. This was a far cry from the amounts the merchants were requesting. Beleaguered by the merchants' constant demands, Government Exchange House officials gradually began to change larger amounts: two, five; ten, and as much as thirty dollars for a privileged few on rare occasions. These arbitrary exchange limits inevitably invited confusion.

On the morning of August 22 two officials at the Government Exchange House were sitting in front of a box of ichibus and drinking tea, as was their unvarying custom at the beginning of the working day. Although limits had been placed on the exchange requests of foreign merchants, the officials had the box of ichibus ready so that they could supply them.

That day their first visitor was British Vice-Consul Vyse, who came striding in unannounced, accompanied by his interpreter. Vyse immediately began shouting at them, as though he were scolding servants.

"Yesterday I gave my interpreter five hundred dollars to be exchanged for ichibus, but you refused to do it. May I ask why?"

Vyse's interpreter had come in the day before carrying five hundred dollars, which weighed nearly 31 pounds—quite a heavy load—and demanded to exchange them for their equivalent weight in ichibus. "We have to change dollars for other people as well," one official answered. "If you would like to change five hundred dollars, please submit a letter explaining the reason."

"You ask that I submit a letter, but I have already sent one concerning this matter to the governor," said Vyse.

The letter that Vyse had sent the governor of foreign affairs actually had nothing to do with the five hundred dollars. Early that morning the two governors had boarded a small boat flying the black-and-white striped flag of Bakufu patrol boats and headed toward Kanagawa. Knowing that they would not be there to contradict him, Vyse felt safe in making his demands.

"As a high-ranking official, I require five hundred dollars' worth of ichibus. If it pleases you gentlemen, I would like to exchange that amount of dollars today," said Vyse.

The British home government had given detailed instructions to not only Alcock but also the consuls in Nagasaki and Hakone and the vice-consul and interpreters in Kanagawa. These instructions stated that they were strictly forbidden from engaging in trade on their own account or serving as company agents, either directly or indirectly.

At this time no distinction was made between diplomats and merchants. Nearly all European diplomats in the Far East conducted business on the side at their posts of duty. This mixing of business and diplomacy strongly influenced their conduct of public affairs and gave rise to many abuses. England, in line with its friendly policy toward Japan, forbade its diplomats from engaging in trade. In compensation, the British government increased their annual salaries slightly. Many were attracted by these relatively high salaries.

Diplomats were also instructed to avoid disputes with the Japanese people and officials at all costs and to give them no cause to commit aggression.

In addition, they were told to refrain from actions aimed at evading Japanese customs duties or reducing customs revenue; British diplomats in China were at that time doing all of these things openly—to the severe detriment of British-Chinese relations.

Vyse, for example, had been instructed to argue as little as possible with Japanese officials—the reverse of his conduct that day. Also, he was forbidden to engage in trade on his own account, either directly or indirectly, but how else was one to regard the purchase of cobangs? But it was also a temptation almost too strong to resist—and Vyse was not a strong man. So on August 22 he demanded that he be allowed to change five hundred dollars.

The official who dealt with Vyse was Yamashita Kanemon, whose rank as *shirabeyaku*—inspector—made him equivalent to a commissioned military officer. Yamashita passed Vyse's request to his superior, who gave him the following sensible instructions: "Vyse is not a merchant and has a definite need for the money, so there is no harm in changing it for him."

Yamashita therefore told Vyse that he would change the five hundred dollars.

Vyse put his bag on the table, opened it, and raked out the

coins. Yamashita counted them—there were nearly seven hundred dollars—and raised his head:

"There is more than five hundred here. Please take back the extra dollars."

"Why not change them, now that you've got the chance?"

"This is not the amount you mentioned."

"I know, but would you mind holding the remainder for me?"

Vyse's plan was to leave the extra coins and receive ichibus for them later.

Nine English merchants were watching this scene intently. Hearing that their vice-consul had left for the Government Exchange House to change a large amount of dollars, they had scurried after him and managed to witness the entire exchange.

"If the vice-consul can change five hundred dollars, we should be allowed to change one hundred dollars each," interjected J. S. Barber who, together with William Keswick, represented Jardine, Matheson & Company in Yokohama.

"Yes," said Vyse, embarrassed that he had been singled out for preferential treatment, "let them change one hundred dollars."

Tanaka Konoshin, who was one rank lower than Yamashita and in charge of accounting and general affairs, came forward to take care of the merchants' requests. He had never changed money for nine foreigners at once, let alone in amounts of one hundred dollars each. Tanaka and Yamashita consulted with another official.

They decided that, because the vice-consul had interceded on the merchants' behalf, they would permit all nine to change fifty dollars each.

"We will allow the merchants to change fifty dollars," Tanaka announced.

Although the firm of Jardine, Matheson had rather recently acquired a reputation for civilized behavior, twenty years before its employees had been known for their rough-and-ready ways—

and unscrupulous business tactics. When it came to cobang profiteering, Barber was a throwback—and didn't care who knew it.

"If you allow the acting consul five hundred dollars, why do we get only fifty?" he asked, stepping toward Tanaka.

"That is what we have decided," said Tanaka flatly.

"Under whose authority do you refuse our request? What's your name?" Barber asked insultingly. Stepping forward, he made as though to grab Tanaka by the front of his coat.

"Tanaka Konoshin," replied Tanaka reluctantly. Before Barber could touch him, he rose to his knees and grabbed the hilt of his sword.

"Stand back, you!" he shouted.

When European diplomats had first come to China and Siam, they had not concerned themselves very much with the ranks of their negotiating partners. Occasionally, they negotiated with low-ranking officials who treated them with contempt. As a result, the Treaty of Nanking expressly stated the right of British diplomats to directly communicate on a basis of equality with Chinese officials of similar rank.

Diplomats had also experienced this contempt in Japan. When the diplomatic corps was in Yokohama, Alcock, representing the others, had asked the Japanese to regard foreign ministers as equal to ministers of foreign affairs, and foreign consuls and vice-consuls as equal to governors of foreign affairs.

The Japanese immediately acquiesced; they, as well as Harris and Alcock, had desired such a clarification.

Japanese society was layered into strictly graded ranks; the Japanese thus found it difficult to deal with someone of undefined standing. It was only natural that they would need to establish the relative status of foreign diplomats vis-à-vis their own officials. When they opened the ports, they assumed that the status of foreign merchants was as low as their own. Bakufu officials were samurai and ranked far above mere merchants. Accordingly, when they dealt with foreign merchants, these officials regarded them as they did their Japanese counterparts.

They thought of them as *shirasu*: men who groveled on the *shirasu*—the white gravel spread in front of the veranda of a typical samurai home.

"Where are you from? What business brings you here?" the samurai would disdainfully inquire of a petitioning merchant, making him kneel before him on the gravel.

That image of the humble merchant bowing to the proud samurai—repeated over and over—was firmly fixed in the samurai mind. But when the ports opened, the foreign merchants, as well as the ships' captains and crew, had come together with the vice-consuls, who were said to hold the same rank as a Japanese governor of foreign affairs. It made no sense.

"Hey, you! Merchants can't enter here. Get back on the *shirasu*!" the officials would shout.

But the foreigners laughed and ignored them. Even the big dogs they brought, which the Japanese called *kame*—mistaking the command "come on" for their name—paid no attention to rank. Thrusting forth muzzles that seemed to be as big as their bodies, they were completely undisciplined. The patience of the Bakufu officials was wearing dangerously thin.

Now this Barber, a mere merchant, had taken this same high-handed attitude toward one of those officials—Tanaka. No matter how slight and spindly his appearance, Tanaka was still a samurai. The blood rushed to his head. He gripped the hilt of his sword.

"Enough of your impudence. Stand back!"

Yamashita struck the same threatening pose. Realizing that they would not hesitate to cut him down, Barber retreated. A silence fell over the room. But Tanaka had a wife and child in Edo. If he drew his sword—even by mistake—and caused an incident, he would have to commit *seppuku*—ritual suicide. What would happen to his family then? Tanaka relaxed his grip.

"In any case, we'd like to leave our dollars with you," said Vyse. One of the merchants picked up the wooden box, which had fallen over. Vyse put in seven hundred dollars, and the merchants, one hundred apiece. They then nailed the lid shut and leaving the box with the officials, departed.

Of course, they intended to eventually receive ichibus for the dollars they had left behind.

✳

Alcock soon heard from Vyse about the incident.

"It never would have happened if the Japanese had not imposed limits on the exchange of ichibus," said Vyse, not mentioning the real cause: his request to change five hundred dollars so that he could speculate in cobangs. Alcock, however, believed him completely. After hearing Vyse's account of this incident, Alcock repeatedly demanded that Tanaka and Yamashita be punished.

To Alcock, the recent behavior of the Japanese government—the withdrawal of the nishu, the decision to allow the free exchange of ichibus, the sudden imposition of exchange limits soon after—showed maddening inconstancy.

Even though it's been two months since the opening of the ports, trade has made absolutely no progress, he thought.

Alcock had told the Japanese he had no intention of discussing the currency question. He had left that to Harris, as the senior diplomat. Recently Harris had told him that the Japanese government was deliberately delaying his audience with the Tycoon.

Harris's manner toward me has cooled, thought Alcock. The man is putting me off with polite phrases and taking no action at all on the currency question.

Because Alcock had said he had no intention of discussing the currency question with the Japanese, he felt it was up to Harris to do something. The Japanese, of course, wanted to maintain the status quo. Just when Alcock's anger was about to boil over, along came the report from Vyse. Alcock immediately left for the American legation to prod Harris into action.

After Alcock's visit—and polite scolding—Harris paid a call on Manabe Akikatsu, the Prince of Sabae and a minister of foreign affairs, on August 27, five days after Vyse's attempt to change dollars at Yokohama.

This was Harris's second visit to Manabe at his official residence since coming to Edo. He had last seen him at their meeting about a month ago.

There was one other minister of foreign affairs—the newly appointed Wakisaka Yasuori, the Prince of Tatsuno. This was Harris's first meeting with Wakisaka. Today both Manabe and Wakisaka had come to greet Harris.

Harris's first impulse was to protest his treatment by the Japanese. He began speaking about the currency question, as he had been asked to by Alcock, but his thoughts soon began to drift in another direction.

"Ever since coming to Edo, I have experienced a great deal of ill feeling directed toward me. My recent promotion to the rank of minister by the President of the United States—the appointment, in other words, of a minister to Japan instead of a consul general—should be regarded as an expression of respect for the Tycoon. Since my appointment, however, no one has come to congratulate me on my safe arrival at my new post or invited me to celebrate my promotion. The only Japanese officials to come to the legation have been low in rank. Although two months have already passed, I have yet to meet with any high-ranking officials. Instead, I have been treated like a cipher—the lowest of the low."

Harris had negotiated the treaty with Hotta Masayoshi, the Prince of Sakura, who was then serving as prime minister and minister of foreign affairs. Hotta was the most progressive Japanese of his generation. If Harris had wanted, he could have easily visited Hotta at the residences of high officials anytime he wished.

But around the time the commercial treaty was signed, a change of government occurred and Hotta was deposed. In his place, Ii Naosuke, the Prince of Hikone, an arch-conservative whose views were diametrically opposed to Hotta's, became the de facto prime minister.

Harris was dimly aware of this political struggle but did not know the details. And no one was willing to tell him. The Japanese kept their dealings with foreign countries separate from domestic political quarrels. Harris had come to Japan believing that there was no difference between progressive and conservative factions in their attitude toward foreigners.

Harris, a bachelor, was a sociable man. As a minister, the highest diplomatic rank, Harris had come to Edo expecting to enjoy the society of Japanese nobles, high-ranking government officials, and their families. But a conservative like Ii would never consider social intercourse with foreigners. Because Harris had come to Edo of his own free will, Ii did not find it necessary to send an official to congratulate him on his arrival at his post. Harris, however, had been wounded by this treatment, and his conversation naturally turned in that direction.

Hotta had been an exception. Most Japanese felt that not only Harris and Alcock but all foreigners were unwanted guests. Moreover, western-style social functions were unknown to them. In any event, they could not imagine socializing with someone like Harris.

Manabe wondered what Harris was trying to say—his complaints made no sense at all. When Harris paused, Manabe brought the discussion back to firmer ground: "About the currency problem you mentioned earlier . . ."

Now it was Harris's turn to be confused: after Manabe's opening remarks, he had no idea what the man was talking about.

Ministers of foreign affairs were appointed from the Roju— the five or six members of the council of state. The Roju were midlevel *daimyos*, or feudal lords, chosen from a small number of select families. The pool of qualified candidates was thus small as well. The capable Hotta had been a rare exception: nearly all the other Roju were merely putting in time, with no innate talent for their work. Manabe was typical. He had no intention of giving Harris a straightforward answer; his only thought was evasion.

"We *daimyo* are not used to dealing with money. We have ordered the official in charge to handle this matter so that there will be no further misunderstanding. We have also asked that official to attend this meeting today."

Harris abruptly broke in, saying, "What's the point of having the official in charge be present today? The currency question has already been dealt with in the treaty. There is no reason to involve the official in charge."

When Hotta had been prime minister and minister of foreign affairs, the Bakufu had appointed many capable bureaucrats and made the most of their talents. These officials opposed Ii's appearance on the same political stage. When Ii took power, he purged them and installed instead the current crowd of incompetents.

One of the governors of foreign affairs was Mizuno Tadanori, the Prince of Chikugo. Mizuno had been demoted for criticizing Hotta's foreign policy as being too radical. This, as it turned out, had been a lucky stroke for him: he was later rehabilitated by Ii and made a governor of foreign affairs. Mizuno, rather than the two incompetent ministers of foreign affairs, was the one who was really in charge of foreign diplomacy.

Mizuno dealt with all diplomatic problems, including the most pressing: currency. The minting and circulation of the nishu had been Mizuno's work. In the name of the ministers of foreign affairs, he had also handled the correspondence with Harris and Alcock concerning the currency question.

Although he had said that the official in charge would be present at the meeting, Manabe suddenly remembered that Mizuno was in Yokohama, not Edo. There was no one else present who could negotiate the currency question with Harris. Manabe tried to wriggle out of his predicament by saying, "Discussing this matter would take a long time, so we would like to put our proposal in a letter. We Japanese are still not used to seeing dollars in circulation, so some inconvenience is unavoidable. But as we become accustomed to them, the present barriers to trade will surely disappear. The government will provide various kinds of guidance to hasten that process."

Article Five, which stated that currency could be exchanged weight for weight, contained the following proviso: "As some time will elapse before the Japanese will be acquainted with the value of foreign coin, the Japanese government will, for the period of one year after the opening of the harbor, furnish the Americans with Japanese coins, equal weights being given and no discount taken for recoinage."

This could be taken to mean that when the Japanese became acquainted with foreign currency, they would no longer have to change it.

Before leaving for Yokohama, Mizuno had said that Japanese officials, using this proviso as a pretext, could refuse to change money for foreign merchants. This is what Manabe meant by "provide various kinds of guidance."

Harris, however, loudly insisted that limiting the exchange of dollars was a violation of the treaty. Once again, Manabe retreated in confusion, saying, "As I mentioned earlier, we Japanese *daimyo* are not used to handling money. Therefore, I will order the official in charge to conduct an investigation and when it is completed, send you our proposal in a letter."

Harris, who had turned away from Manabe in disgust, spun around sharply. "I have been inquiring about this matter for some time now, but all you can do is repeat '*daimyo, daimyo,*' like a parrot. I don't know how high-ranking a *daimyo* is supposed to be, but I would expect that, since coming here, you have had time to become acquainted with the gist of the treaty. Or perhaps you have not. And yet you can still perform your duties as minister of foreign affairs? I envy you. It must be splendid to remain ignorant and still retain one's post."

Manabe bitterly resented Harris's sarcasms, a seriously insulting form of address to Japanese ears. His subordinates in the foreign office ground their teeth in embarrassment as they heard Harris's words.

"I am a *daimyo*. I don't know anything" soon became a catchphrase among the lower-ranking officials in the Foreign Affairs Office.

✳

Manabe had repeatedly referred to "the official in charge." As he listened to Manabe's explanation, Harris understood that this "official in charge" had to be the Prince of Chikugo and the governor of foreign affairs: Mizuno. He also realized that Mizuno was the mastermind behind the Japanese government's currency policy.

About one month previously Harris had visited Manabe at his official residence. In his conversation with Harris, Manabe had claimed that the nishu was a legitimate currency. Harris was now convinced that Mizuno was Manabe's puppeteer. He had told him what to say, from beginning to end. Now that foreigners were no longer fooled by the Bakufu's scheme to triple the price of goods, Mizuno had gone to Yokohama to take personal command of the situation and halt the exchange of ichibus.

Mizuno was still in Yokohama and had not been present at Harris's second meeting with Manabe. Manabe had repeatedly said the official in charge would attend, but not one of the governors of foreign affairs seated behind him had given him a word of support. The mastermind had to be the Prince of Chikugo.

Harris told Alcock his conclusion that the Prince of Chikugo must be the power behind the throne at the Foreign Affairs Office.

Alcock had met Mizuno once, at the ceremony to exchange ratifications. He remembered him as having doubled-lidded eyes and a defiant look, like an unruly boy in a man's body. And now Harris was saying that this man was directing the Bakufu's currency policy.

Though Alcock did not know how much power Mizuno wielded in the government or how he had pushed himself to the forefront, he could recall certain incidents that supported Harris's description of the man as a "mastermind." As Harris told his story, Alcock found himself agreeing with one part after another. Although Mizuno had impressed him as a charming fellow, Alcock now saw that his charm was a cover for slyness and trickery.

How can we eliminate this man, Alcock wondered. How can we have him dismissed? Now Alcock had another, highly vexing diplomatic problem to handle. Furthermore, Vyse and his merchant friends had caused an uproar over their demand to change dollars for ichibus. Based on Vyse's slanted version of the incident, Alcock began to press for the dismissal of not only Tanaka and Yamashita but Mizuno and another governor of foreign affairs, who were responsible for supervising their subordinates at the government customshouse, although he did not have a strong case against the latter two. Just then, however, an incident occurred in Yokohama that made Alcock's demand for the Prince of Chikugo's dismissal seem more reasonable.

※

Wars cost money. When the Arrow War broke out, the British public had violently opposed dispatching warships, partly because of the cost. England and the United States both had small governments, with budgets small enough to be comprehensible to ordinary people; they had not yet grown to unimaginable proportions. Unlike today, the general public was extremely sensitive to how those budgets were spent.

Overcoming public opposition, the British government had appropriated great sums of money, dispatched warships, and finally bullied China into signing the Treaty of Tientsin.

At the same time, the Russian commander in Siberia, Count Nikolai Nikolaevich Muraviyov, had obtained an enormous tract of territory in Manchuria from China through the Treaty of Aigun. Russia was then pursuing a policy of national expansion. From the standpoint of national benefit, the achievement of Muraviyov, whose only aim had been to obtain land, was much more important than that of Eufimy Puchachin, who had negotiated the treaties of Tientsin and Edo. These treaties, rooted as they were in the philosophy of free trade, meant little to Russia, which had little interest in foreign trade.

Commanding a squadron of seven warships, Muraviyov had sailed into Yokohama the week before Vyse and his friends had caused an incident by attempting to buy large sums of ichibus. Muraviyov had come to Japan to negotiate the Japanese-Russian boundary on Sakhalin Island. After stopping briefly in Yokohama, he had proceeded to Edo with four warships. Ten days later, on August 25, a total of six Russian warships—three that Muraviyov had left behind and three that had arrived later— were anchored in Yokohama harbor.

At nine o'clock on the evening of that day, three Russians who had come ashore to purchase supplies—an officer, a sailor, and a steward—were suddenly attacked on their way back to the ship, near the temporary lodgings for foreigners next to the customshouse. Twenty Americans—members of an exploration and survey expedition who had lost their ship in a typhoon— were staying in the lodgings. The assassins' real target might well have been the Americans. If so, the Russians were simply unlucky.

The steward was the first to be attacked but found refuge in a vegetable store, where he had just finished shopping. The officer and sailor, however, were caught and cut down. Many foreigners would later be murdered by Japanese in Yokohama, Edo, and the resort town of Kamakura. This was the first of such incidents.

On receiving word of the murders, the three vice-consuls in Kanagawa boarded a small boat and hurried to Yokohama, guided by the faint lights on shore. At the customshouse they found a bonfire burning and, nearby, the two bodies laid out on the ground. The consuls brought their paper lanterns closer to better view the wounds. Both bodies had been hacked mercilessly.

The sight was so ghastly that Vyse's voice wavered uncontrollably as he called for someone to get the *bugyo*—the governor of foreign affairs. A Japanese official who happened to be present informed him that the *bugyo* never came to the customshouse.

"What?" shouted Vyse, now enraged. "Go find him right now!" He had expected the *bugyo* to come running.

In the northern section of Yokohama there was a small hill overlooking a large cove. On top of the hill was the Kanagawa *bugyo's*, or magistrate's, office. The governors of foreign affairs also served as Kanagawa *bugyo* and stayed at the Kanagawa *bugyo*'s office while in Yokohama. One of those *bugyo*, the "mastermind" Mizuno, was at the Kanagawa *bugyo's* office that night.

A customshouse official, bearing the request of the three vice-consuls that the *bugyo* come right away, hurried off to the Kanagawa *bugyo's* office. After a short while, he returned with a message from Mizuno: "He said to inform the official in charge and have him deal with the matter."

All three vice-consuls voiced their anger at this reply, but to no avail.

The criminals had vanished into thin air, leaving no definite clues. Foreigners in Yokohama, including the consuls, claimed the initial investigation had been bungled by the apparently unconcerned *bugyo*. They harshly criticized Mizuno for not rushing to the scene.

"Maybe the *bugyo* himself was in on it," they said. Their anger was further fueled by Mizuno's continued restrictions on the exchange of ichibus. They directed a steady stream of abuse at the *bugyo* and sent an official letter to Edo detailing their complaints.

Alcock had been waiting for something like this. Using negligence in the murder investigation as a reason, he could now openly demand Mizuno's resignation. He asked Harris to join him and tried to persuade Muraviyov as well. Encouraged by Alcock, Muraviyov also called for Mizuno's ouster.

※

Until now Manabe had left the currency question completely in Mizuno's hands. Just as he had told Harris, he had never dealt with filthy lucre—such matters really were beneath a *daimyo* like himself. He had also never wondered whether what Mizuno was telling him was wrong or right. He had concluded that if Mizuno, an experienced foreign service officer, had said so, then that was good enough for him.

Mizuno's apparent tricks, such as his attempt to triple prices for foreigners, had caused the foreign representatives to label Manabe a charlatan and a crook. When Harris had called on Manabe the second time, he had not only rebuked him but mocked him ("I don't know how high ranking a *daimyo* is supposed to be . . .") in front of the governors of foreign affairs and other lower-ranking officials.

Lying its way out of tight spots had been the Bakufu's preferred method of conducting foreign affairs ever since the arrival of Perry, as Manabe well knew. He had often used it himself in his battles with foreign representatives. Manabe again reflected on Mizuno's approach to the currency question. He realized that Mizuno would not hesitate to lie to the foreigners, if he thought it would help him out of a predicament.

If Manabe was right—if Mizuno's lies were the cause of his own current troubles—why did he have to be singled out for ridicule, when he was just trying to protect his subordinate?

When Manabe had met Harris for the second time, he had sidestepped the American minister's pesky questions by saying that, because Japan was a small country, it could only change a small number of dollars. "That has nothing to do with it," Harris had replied. "All you have to do is immediately recoin the dollars you receive into ichibus. I strongly advise you to do so."

At first, Manabe had not paid much attention to Harris's suggestion, but soon it began to echo loudly in his mind. Harris was right, of course. All they had to do was recoin the silver dollars they received in weight-for-weight exchange into silver ichibus and pass them off to the foreigners. That way, they would lose nothing.

Mizuno was in Yokohama. Manabe knew that if he consulted him, Mizuno would oppose his decision. And if they argued, Manabe would lose. Fortunately, Mizuno was not around. Manabe began to lean toward adopting Harris's proposal.

It was at that point when the Russian officer and sailor were murdered and the foreign diplomats began to call for Mizuno's dismissal.

If he forced Mizuno to resign, he could put an end to this uproar—and that, finally, is what Manabe decided to do. First, however, he took Ii into his confidence. Then, summoning Alcock, Manabe announced that the Japanese government would recoin dollars into ichibus and exchange 10,000 ichibus a day in Yokohama and 6,000 a day in Nagasaki and Hakodate, weight-for-weight.

✳

The Japanese government began exchanging 10,000 ichibus a day in Yokohama on September 19, eighty days after the opening of the ports.

The foreign merchants' appetite for ichibus was ravenous.

Eager to obtain those magical coins they could transform into fortunes, foreign merchants descended upon the Government Exchange House officials, their eyes glittering. Reeling under the crush, the officials soon caved in to their demands. Manabe had promised Alcock that the Bakufu would exchange 10,000 ichibus a day at Yokohama. But beginning the first day and continuing for the next three or four, officials were harassed into changing from 12,000 to 16,000 ichibus daily.

The number of ichibus handed to foreign merchants skyrocketed. Cobangs, once worth only six ichibus apiece, shot up to eight and nine ichibus, rising by half-ichibu increments. The official rate was one cobang to four ichibus. When the selling price of cobangs rose to eight ichibus, the profit to the Japanese doubled. Cobangs slowly surfaced in Edo and began to flow into Yokohama. The Bakufu moved quickly to prohibit the sale of cobangs to foreigners. But like Vice-Consul Vyse, the Japanese found this trade an opportunity too tempting to resist. By hook or by crook, they began to brings cobangs to Yokohama.

And the foreign merchants rushed to buy them. Like California and Australia before it, Yokohama was burning with gold rush fever. At the Government Exchange House, foreign merchants would write the amount of dollars they wanted to change on a piece of paper. The officials would not necessarily agree to change that amount, but would use it as a reference point. The foreign merchants began presenting written requests for huge sums.

Requests to change two or three million dollars were routine. One merchant handed over a request in the sextillions, a number so high—with twenty-one zeros—that a lifetime wouldn't be long enough to count it.

The Government Exchange House officials countered, ineffectually, by making the merchants sign their requests. The Japanese, however, could not read western languages, a fact of which the merchants were well aware.

At first, they signed using the names of friends and acquaintances, but that soon proved inadequate and bothersome. Some simply wrote nonsense, like Snooks, Tooks, Bosh, Moses, Messrs. Nonsense and Hook'em, Doddard, and Is It Not. But having these men, crazed with a lust for ichibus, sign their names was also nonsense.

When the price of cobangs rose to nine ichibus, the profit the foreign merchants could make fell to fifty percent: too low to make the trade worthwhile. But Japan had the cheapest prices in the world. Goods were extremely inexpensive. Although the prices of goods were climbing steadily, the rise was not as sharp as that of cobangs. Instead of cobangs, which yielded only a fifty percent return, it was much more profitable to buy goods. Although shipping them required time, labor, and money, goods bought in Japan and sold on the China coast brought the same return on capital as cobangs.

Quickly noticing this fact, foreign merchants began to actively buy goods. William Keswick of Jardine, Matheson wrote to the company's Shanghai office concerning the business situation at this time: "The profit on cobangs is only fifty percent, much lower than the profit on silk, marine products, and fish oil."

Foreign merchants began to purchase any and all goods they could get their hands on. Like cobangs before them, goods began to soar in price.

※

The frigate *Powhatan*, the flagship of the American East Indian fleet, sailed into Yokohama on October 3, when the city was still in the grip of gold fever.

Crews aboard American warships served a two-year tour of duty in East Asia. The crew of the *Powhatan* had already passed the two-year mark and was eager to return home. On its way back to the United States, the *Powhatan* had received orders from the United States government to stop in Yokohama and pick up a Japanese diplomatic mission bound for Washington, where they were to exchange treaty ratifications.

The exchange of treaty ratifications between Japan and England had taken place in Japan. It had been decided, however, to exchange ratified treaties between the United States and Japan in Washington.

An American naval officer had been waiting impatiently for the *Powhatan*'s arrival. His name was Lieutenant Charles Thorburn.

Thorburn had arrived in Yokohama at the end of July. He had been the second officer aboard the *Fenimore Cooper*, a survey ship that had been sent to find the best steamship route between San Francisco and Hong Kong. Thorburn had also been the second-in-command of the survey party. The *Fenimore Cooper*, however, had run aground in a typhoon. Because many of her timbers were rotten, she was judged to be not worth repairing and was auctioned off. The *Fenimore Cooper*'s crew numbered twenty-one men. Left without a ship, they had taken up residence at the temporary lodgings for foreigners that the Bakufu had built for foreign merchants in Yokohama.

The gold rush began in Yokohama one month later. Thorburn and the rest of the *Fenimore Cooper*'s crew, however, were observers, rather than participants, in this event.

After reaching the bottom of the *Fenimore Cooper*'s safe, they did not have any dollars to exchange for ichibus. And even had they had money in the safe, a sailor's pay was only twelve dollars a month. With twelve dollars, they could not hope to keep up with the merchants in the hunt for cobang gold.

Thorburn himself was not only penniless but in debt. On returning from Yokohama, he asked the leader of the expedition, John M. Brooke, if he could exchange his food ration for money to pay his debts.

The members of the survey party, including Thorburn, could only look on with envy at the gold rush.

If I only had a few dollars, thought Thorburn. Now the *Powhatan* had finally arrived.

Thorburn lost no time boarding the *Powhatan* and approaching the commodore and officers. "As you can see," he said, "Yokohama is in the middle of a gold rush. Anyone can make all the money he wants. How about it, gentlemen? Would you like to make a fortune?"

The commodore was Josiah Tattnal. When the Anglo-French squadron struck at China's Taku forts, he had towed a British sailing ship out of harm's way, violating his government's policy of neutrality in the Arrow War. Tattnal later said he had done it because Americans were kinsmen of the British and "blood is thicker than water." A stouthearted navy man, Tattnal had suddenly become a well-known, popular figure in European society on the China coast.

"And how can we do that?" asked Tattnal, leaning forward.

"There's nothing to it. All you need are dollars. How many dollars is the *Powhatan* carrying?"

The *Powhatan*'s safe, said Tattnal, was virtually empty.

"Then you should go to Shanghai and get dollars."

Thorburn told them that in Shanghai they could obtain dollars with a note issued by the warship.

"I see," Tattnal replied. The commodore then proceeded to behave in a way that the uninformed could only call strange. And the *Powhatan* was soon to sail a route best described as unusual.

✳

Commodore Tattnal had intended to escort the Japanese emissaries by way of the Cape of Good Hope, the southernmost point on the African continent.

One reason was fuel: on the way, the *Powhatan* could take on coal at the British colonies of Hong Kong, Singapore, Pointe de Galle, and the Mauritius Islands. It could also do the same after leaving Cape Town. But if it returned by way of Cape Horn, the southernmost point of South America, its only coal depot till San Francisco was in Honolulu. Also, after leaving Panama, the Pacific terminus of the American transcontinental railway, it would have to round Cape Horn and sail to Buenos Aires before it could find coal.

Because coal was expensive and steamships consumed great quantities of it, they would set sail when the wind was favorable and would not ordinarily burn coal. But when they were becalmed or when entering and leaving port they would fire up their furnaces and sail under steam power. The Cape of Good Hope route offered plenty of stopping points where they could replenish their supplies of coal. The Cape Horn route did not; it was a long, difficult haul. Except for whaling ships, which pursued their quarry in all seven seas, few, if any, steam-powered warships rounded Cape Horn and crossed over to Asia. The Cape of Good Hope route was standard: Perry had used it when he came to Japan.

Tattnal went to Edo to consult with Harris about escorting the Japanese mission. Harris told Tattnal to take the Cape Horn route.

Harris was a minister; Tattnal, a commodore. Theoretically, they were of the same rank, but a commodore had far greater authority and more subordinates. If Tattnal had rejected Harris's proposal out of hand, that would have been the end of it. But Tattnal quickly agreed to the illogical Pacific route and taking his leave of Harris, returned to Yokohama.

Before sailing for Shanghai, Tattnal told Americans in Yokohama that he planned to leave the city on February 22 of the following year and escort the Japanese mission to Panama by way of the Sandwich Islands and San Francisco. Prior to departure, he would go to Shanghai, load on coal, and return immediately. He would then go to Hong Kong to complete procedures for transferring his command to his successor.

The price of coal in Nagasaki was five dollars a ton—one-third its cost in Shanghai. Although foreign merchants in Nagasaki could change only a limited number of dollars, local authorities, fearing the warships, allowed their crews an exchange rate of three ichibus to the dollar. Russian and American warships thus made a point of regularly stopping for coal at Nagasaki.

Americans there found it exceedingly strange that Tattnal would go to Shanghai to take on coal. Still stranger was his plan to return to Yokohama before sailing on to Hong Kong. It would have made sense to head south to Hong Kong directly from Shanghai.

Americans were still shaking their heads over Tattnal's itinerary when, twenty days later, on October 31, the *Powhatan* returned from Shanghai.

The rumor spread quickly: the *Powhatan* was carrying 450,000 Mexican dollars.

Thorburn took the initiative in negotiating with the governors of foreign affairs, with the full support of Harris, who was in on Tattnall's plan. In return for Tattnall's escorting the Japanese mission to America, the Government Exchange House would permit the *Powhatan* to change its dollars for 150,000 ichibus in one lump sum—a fifteen-day supply for foreign merchants in Yokohama.

News of this largesse soon made the rounds of the foreign community.

Thorburn rushed about buying cobangs like a man possessed. His base of operations was the foreigners' lodgings, where he was staying. Nearly every day, local dealers came pounding on his door in the dead of night calling for *Soru no dana*—"Master Thorburn."

Soon another rumor spread: An American naval officer was diligently buying cobangs every day at the lodgings for foreigners. The thought that an officer on the *Powhatan* had been allowed to purchase fifteen days' worth of ichibus at one time and was now rushing about buying cobangs with them was unbearable to the merchants, who had been living in the lodgings prior to Thorburn's arrival. They erupted with a tremendous howl of protest.

"Let's write letters to the *North!*" they cried. No foreign newspapers were published in Yokohama. For the foreign merchants there, the *North China Herald*, of Shanghai, was the only English-language paper in which they could vent their indignation.

Some of the American merchants shrilly proclaimed that they would "notify the American government."

Thorburn, however, kept on scooping up cobangs in utter indifference to the criticism raining down on him.

Using nearly 90,000 ichibus, he purchased 10,000 cobangs. When the supply of cobangs finally ran out before he could spend 150,000 ichibus, he quickly used the remaining 60,000 to buy Japanese goods.

Cobangs were conveniently compact: Thorburn could easily take his entire hoard aboard the *Powhatan*. The goods, however, were another story. It would not look right for the flagship of the American East India Squadron to sail out of port with all flags flying and commercial cargo stacked to the rails. Instead, Thorburn chartered the schooner *Colneria L. Behan* to transport his cargo.

Observing these antics, Americans in Yokohama easily solved the mystery of why the *Powhatan* had bought coal in Shanghai and then returned to Yokohama, and why Commodore Tattnal had chosen the difficult Cape Horn route.

He had, of course, gone to Shanghai to obtain dollars—the seeds of the money tree. He had then come back to Yokohama to purchase cobangs and would sail to Hong Kong to sell them, on the pretext of completing procedures for transferring his command to his successor. He had chosen the Pacific route so that after he then retraced his path north to Yokohama to board the Japanese envoys, he could set out directly across the Pacific without returning south to Hong Kong.

The day after the departure of the *Powhatan*, a menacing column of smoke appeared in the skies over Edo. With no wind to disperse it, the smoke rose straight up in a solid mass.

The citizens of Yokohama, both Japanese and foreign, streamed into the Bund, which offered an unobstructed view of the column.

The Japanese and foreigners came to the same conclusion: Edo was burning.

"What part of Edo?" whispered an anxious Japanese who had just come from the capital.

By evening the fire was huge. The sky over the city had turned a darkly glowing red. Just then, the first news arrived from Edo.

"The *donjon* of the castle has been destroyed by the fire," said the Japanese to one another.

"The Tycoon's palace has burnt to the ground," said the foreigners.

Alcock watched the holocaust from the deck of the corvette Highflyer, *on its way from Edo to Kanagawa. "Good Lord," he said to the man on his right, the consul posted at Hakodate, "how in God's name will they survive it?" The blaze indeed appeared to be ravaging the city.*

"Many won't, of course," responded the consul, who fancied himself something of a student of things Japanese. "But frightful fires have been commonplace throughout the city's history—all that wood, the paper lanterns, earthquakes . . . they even have a rather morbid nickname for them," he said, pausing. "They call the fires the Flowers of Edo."

Alcock shuddered. These people surely had a callous disregard for human life, he thought disdainfully; the bestial murders of the two Russians had demonstrated that.

The British consul felt at this point that he was beginning to achieve the proper note of firmness with the sly, inexplicably changeable Japanese. He was energetically campaigning for the dismissal of the two customshouse officials who had insulted Vice-Consul Vyse. He also felt that the same fate was in store for the "mastermind," Mizuno, who both Alcock and Harris believed was behind the many wily Japanese schemes to thwart the opening of the country to foreign trade.

Of course, the behavior of his fellow Occidentals had not been exemplary, either. Alcock had heard rumors of the greed-crazed rush to speculate in cobangs, extending even to the captain of the American ship Powhatan, *which had escorted the first Japanese envoys to the United States. It was in order to attend to this matter that Alcock was traveling to Kanagawa on the* Highflyer. *Alcock hated this speculative frenzy. It was not only unseemly and immoral, but dangerous: if the Japanese saw the foreigners as parasites sucking their national lifeblood, they would use any means available—including murder—to rid themselves of the pests. And in some cases, Alcock thought darkly, they might well be justified.*

4

Intimidation

A lcock had been absent from Edo for about one month. Hearing of the gold rush in Yokohama, he had boarded the *Highflyer*, a British warship that happened to be in port, and headed for Hakodate, a port on Japan's northern frontier, to inspect the situation there.

When he returned to Edo at the end of October, Alcock was greeted by a list of grievances that Vice-Consul Vyse had forwarded from merchants in Yokohama.

"The officials will only exchange a small number of ichibus."

"The officials allot ichibus without rhyme or reason."

"They delay distribution until we are provoked beyond endurance."

Alcock finished reading Vyse's report, his lips drawn into a mirthless grin. "What it comes down to, sir, is that these merchants are speculating in cobangs," said Alcock's secretary and interpreter, who had presented him with the report. He had served as diplomatic representative in Alcock's absence.

One extremely vital task of Alcock and other British diplomats was to serve as advance agents for British firms: in every corner of the globe, they were busy promoting the sales of goods exported by British businessmen from all over England. The nation's economic existence depended on their labors. Alcock's paramount duty in Japan was to ensure that commercial activities got underway as quickly as possible. Now, four months had passed since the opening of the ports and trade had yet to begin,

71

thought Alcock bitterly. It was all because of those merchants, whose only thought was to fill their own coffers in the rush for cobangs, and everything else be damned.

Alcock was mistaken: foreign merchants would by this time no longer deign to look at cobangs, which had become too expensive. Instead, they had switched to speculation in Japanese goods, which offered a far greater rate of return. Except for uninformed newcomers like the officers on the *Powhatan*, no one showed any interest in cobangs. Alcock, who had been absent from Edo a long time, did not yet know this. But he had already encountered the anger of the foreign merchants.

Alcock wondered how he could stop cobang profiteering. He decided that that problem was first on his agenda.

Soon another foreigner was murdered in Yokohama. The victim was the Chinese servant of the French vice-consul, who was also an agent for Dent and Company. The French chargé d'affaires, Duchesne de Bellecourt, had not come to Japan with a vice-consul for Kanagawa. Instead he had appointed the agent of Dent and Company, a Mr. Loureiro, to the post.

On November 6, Loureiro's Chinese servant had been cut down in broad daylight. In Yokohama's European community it was rumored that he had been killed because he was wearing western-style clothes and had been mistaken for a European.

No one had yet come forward to identify the murderers of the Russian officer and sailor: the case was still a mystery. In the current case as well, there were no known clues that might lead to an arrest. Like the previous case, it would probably remain unsolved.

Europeans in Yokohama were easy targets for murderous Japanese. They had to face the possibility of an encounter with an avenging sword of doom every day. How could they protect themselves? How could they make Japanese authorities in Yokohama, who neglected their duties and displayed little interest in catching criminals, improve security for foreigners?

Alcock and Harris not only had to deal with the currency question but also with the problems of the open ports and the issue of substituting Kanagawa for Yokohama as the open port mentioned in the treaties.

In their negotiations with the Bakufu, they managed to secure a site in Kanagawa for an open port.

But the foreign merchants were indifferent to questions of ghettoization or diplomatic pride: they preferred to settle in Yokohama because it had a deeper harbor, good port facilities already in place, and open land on which to build homes for themselves. For the most part, the practical-minded business-men were no more interested in cultural exchanges with the Japanese than the Japanese were with them.

Jardine, Matheson rented lot number one, the lot closest to the customshouse. Number two was taken by Walsh, Hall and Company, an American firm, number three, by Textor & Co., another American firm, and numbers four and five, by the large French firm, Dent and Company. Employing Japanese carpen-ters, merchants quickly began to build makeshift godowns, or warehouses, in the Japanese style.

Should the foreign merchants settle in Yokohama, the Jap-anese would achieve their aim, which would also mean a com-plete loss of face for foreign diplomats. Somehow, they had to change the site of the open port to Kanagawa.

Yokohama as yet had no hotels. And even had there been one, Alcock would not have stayed there; he had no intention of lend-ing credibility to Yokohama as the legitimate open port. He found a room in the British consulate at Jyoryuji Temple instead.

Beginning the next morning, Alcock set out nearly every day for Yokohama. The Japanese officials he met there had one complaint after another, accompanied by documents proving that foreigners had tried to change huge amounts of dollars, signing ridiculous names that mocked the Japanese, and bought cobangs with the ichibus they had received.

Three days after the fire, the vice-consul received the fol-lowing notice from the *bugyo*: "Because of the palace fire, the government will incur various expenses, which may mean that no ichibus will be sent from Edo. In that event, we may have to refuse to exchange ichibus for the time being."

The next day the minister of foreign affairs sent the same notice to Alcock. Just as the notice warned, the Government Exchange House shut its doors soon afterward. With its closing, the demand for ichibus, which had been growing for some time, escalated even further. The foreign merchants not only pressured the vice-consuls but gathered at the entrance of the Government Exchange House to heap abuse on the Japanese authorities and their policies.

These are the crazed, ravenous dregs of Europe, thought Alcock, pained by the spectacle.

※

After a stay of several days in Yokohama, Alcock returned to Edo. On arriving, he immediately wrote a long official letter to Vyse, with the intention of having it circulated among the British merchants in Yokohama.

> Using the palace fire as a pretext, the Japanese government has decided to suspend the exchange of ichibus. This is, to all practical purposes, the same as suspending trade. Foreign residents, by their unlawful and immoral actions; i.e., their buying of gold coins, must bear the responsibility for reducing trade to this state. Because of their speculations in gold coins, the Japanese government has suspended the exchange of ichibus to prevent this state of affairs from continuing. But it is for you in the exercise of the authority with which you are legally invested in the interest of both nations to punish all those whose acts tend to turn such authority into contempt.

Unbeknownst to Alcock, foreign merchants had already stopped buying cobangs, and in any case, such purchases were not prohibited by the treaty. Furthermore, the proviso of the currency article stated that "coins of all description (with the exception of Japanese copper coin) may be exported from Japan . . ."

Neither the export of cobangs nor the preliminary stages—the search for and purchase of cobangs—violated the treaty in the slightest. British subjects felt that Vyse had no right to punish them for the "crimes" Alcock outlined in his letter.

> It is difficult to say whether the indecent levity, or the disregard of all Treaty conditions and national interests or repute, equally manifested, are most worthy of reprehension. Some are a positive disgrace to anyone bearing the name of an Englishman or having a character to lose. Not only the sums in their preposterous amount, are an insult to the Japanese Government to whose officers these requisitions were presented, but they are documents essentially false and dishonest as purporting to be the names of individuals having a real existence and entitled to demand facilities for Trade; whereas mere words are used as names and made to convey gross and offensive comments. That there be no question upon the strict correctness of this description, I annex true copies of several of these documents so disgraceful to the authors; and I direct you to circulate those, together with a copy of this Despatch for general information among the British Subjects at your port.

The documents, which were requests signed with fabricated names, were unquestionably fraudulent. But Alcock's suggestion that they be made public was disproportionate to the crime. Alcock continued, writing, "yet large sums have been shipped and exported by Foreigners contrary to the stipulations of the Treaties, without manifest or declaration at the Custom House."

Gold coins could be freely and legally imported and exported. They were not subject to customs duty. Although it could be argued that a manifest or declaration was necessary, there was no mention of that in the treaty. In any event, the export of gold coins without either could not be called an illegal act.

> The Japanese have taken the most effective
> means for the moment of protecting themselves, by
> stopping the issue of ichibus, on which the purchase
> of cobangs hangs, and when it is found possible to
> induce the Government to recommence the issue of
> silver at Yokohama, it will at the same time be neces-
> sary to have a clear understanding with the Govern-
> ment and Treasury Department, as to the adoption
> of some intelligible system, and a rigid adherence to
> an equitable principle of distribution, under guaran-
> tees that all who are entitled to apply, shall receive
> impartially a fair share or proportion.

In short, Alcock was instructing Vyse to devise a new system
that would bring about the resumption of legitimate ichibu
exchange. A system, in other words, that would put an end to
the rush for cobangs.

> But it is the business and the duty of all Foreign
> Representatives to prevent a few individuals thus en-
> dangering the relations and damaging the permanent
> interests of nations. . . . It is an imperative duty
> therefore to send out of the country all who lend
> themselves to such mischievous practices, before the
> worse comes of it, and you are directed to keep a
> vigilant eye upon every British subject within your
> jurisdiction and apply the law without hesitation or
> delay in every case of deliberate offense or misde-
> meanor for which legal penalty has been provided.

In his closing remarks, Alcock described the British merchants in Yokohama as though they were criminals.

But even after sending off this letter, Alcock still couldn't
rest easy. Though he had ordered Vyse to punish wrongdoers,
Alcock had his doubts as to how the buying of cobangs violated
the law. He had denounced it as though it did, but he had no
conclusive proof that it was indeed a criminal act. Certainly it
was a moral, if not a legal, offense. Alcock thus tried to appeal

to public opinion in the open ports on the China coast. By doing so, he hoped to impose discipline on the foreign merchants in Yokohama. Alcock applied to the resident minister in China for permission to print his letter to Vyse and Vyse's reply in the *North China Herald*. Permission was granted and the letter was printed.

✳

"The foreign merchants in Yokohama are bad enough, but the Japanese government . . . ," wrote Alcock, bursting with righteous indignation toward not only the foreign traders but also his hosts.

Before leaving Nagasaki, Alcock had made the local authorities agree to address the complaints of British merchants and implement reforms beginning July 1, the day the ports were scheduled to open. But the British consul in Nagasaki reported that nothing had been done about the complaints and that the situation had not improved in the slightest.

Manabe had told Alcock that the Bakufu would permit the exchange of 10,000 ichibus in Yokohama and 6,000 each in Hakodate and Nagasaki. Although some ichibus were sent to Nagasaki, shipments were sporadic, and the amounts much smaller than promised. Even though the ports were, in theory, to have been completely opened on July 1, trade in Nagasaki had gotten under way by fits and starts and had shown hardly any real development.

And as for Kanagawa . . . Alcock had frequently requested that customs be transferred there. He knew that if the customshouse were in Kanagawa, the open port designated in the treaty, foreign and Japanese merchants would naturally move there. The Bakufu replied that foreign and Japanese merchants were free to live anywhere in the area designated by the treaty, but it did not move customs. And the foreign merchants showed a decided preference for Yokohama. In the end, the efforts of Alcock and the other foreign representatives to prevent Yokohama being transformed into another Dejima were a tilt at a windmill—so much wasted energy. They completely lost face.

Alcock realized that the same thing was happening with the currency question.

The Japanese government had at first limited the exchange of ichibus to 10,000 a day. And even though that was far from satisfactory, they finally suspended the exchange of ichibus altogether, explaining that it was a temporary measure necessitated by the palace fire. Of course that was just an excuse.

His patience had also been sorely tried by the Bakufu's decision to allow the crew of the *Powhatan* to buy 150,000 ichibus. And then there was the problem of Japanese officials needlessly meddling in the trade between foreign and Japanese merchants. In modern terms, this meddling by Japanese customs officials constituted a nontariff barrier. In other words, it hampered free trade and violated the treaties.

Such problems seemed endless, and the numerous incidents they occasioned further provoked Alcock's ire.

The evening that Alcock set out for Kanagawa, an express messenger came from Edo bearing a letter signed by both ministers of foreign affairs. "Documents have become scattered and lost because of the recent fire. Therefore, they may be a delay in replying to your inquiries. We request your understanding," it said. Alcock knew that the ministers were doubtless busy, but on November 17 he requested an interview with them. Two days later two governors of foreign affairs came to the British mission.

Alcock told them that he wished to "meet with the ministers of foreign affairs in the near future." There was, however, no reply. On the 24th, Alcock pressed for an answer. None came. On the 30th he again demanded a response, to no avail.

Using the pretext of the palace fire to close the Government Exchange House had been had enough, but now the ministers of foreign affairs gave the same excuse to avoid meeting him. Was there any other country like this in the world? Was it not exactly the same as China?

Now that he thought about it, Alcock realized that Manabe was playing the part of Yeh. The arrogant, unapproachable Yeh, who expressed neither wonder nor admiration, and the emaciated, ascetic-looking Manabe, an old man with a gloomy face that never clearly showed what he was feeling, had at least one thing in common: no aptitude for diplomacy.

Alcock recalled his instructions. "The British government," Lord Malmesbury had written, "must rely on your judgment to win the confidence of the Japanese people regarding British intentions toward them. You must be content with gradual progress and not exert pressure for immediate compliance with your suggestions or demands. You should insist on the fulfillment of the provisions of the Treaty of Edo, but not in a manner calculated to give offense to the Japanese government."

Of course, he had no choice but to obey the instructions. That was a diplomat's first duty. But without the backing of military force, how could he compel observance of the treaty from Japan, a country that was identical to China in its recalcitrance?

Just when Alcock had reached the limit of his patience, a reply signed by both ministers of foreign affairs arrived. It was nothing but a list of excuses for the delay in responding. "We would like you to meet with the vice ministers, who are second in rank after us."

Alcock's anger finally exploded. He quickly took up his pen:

> To arrive at a harmonious solution, I am prepared to meet with all officials who are entrusted with foreign affairs at any time, now or in the future. These officials must, however, at all times possess the final authority for deciding various matters during the course of our discussions. They must, in other words, have the same authority that you yourselves possess. If they do not have this authority, it would be meaningless for them to meet me, as I possess the plenipotentiary powers of the British Government.

Alcock continued: "Whether peace and tranquility between our two countries can be preserved or whether we enter into a state of war will depend in part on the outcome of our meeting that day."

Alcock had finally played his trump card by mentioning the word *war*. "A violation of the treaty and a state of war between our two countries will lead to serious consequences and reduce Japan's entire administrative organization to a condition of chaos."

In other words, Alcock was suggesting that if talks with the vice ministers, who did have not powers equivalent to his own, broke down, Britain and Japan might enter into a state of war. If that should happen, Japan would fall into chaos and the Japanese would have no one to blame but themselves. Here, Alcock clearly violated his instructions.

✳

Now that the flow of cobangs out of the country, the rush to buy goods, and the rise in prices had caused a crisis, the minister responsible, Manabe, was placed under severe pressure by the tyrant Ii Naosuke, who as Tairo, or regent, was the Bakufu's highest-ranking official.

Manabe had been among Ii's most loyal subordinates ever since Ii had first seized power. The year before, Manabe had gone to Kyoto, arrested men suspected of opposing Ii, and sent them to Edo. Even so, Manabe was a *daimyo*. He did not know anything about financial dealings. But Ii demanded results and began pressuring Manabe to produce them.

Then came the fire at the palace *donjon*. Using the fire as a pretext, Manabe stopped the supply of ichibus—the cause of all the uproar. After that, however, he was at a loss as to how to proceed. Manabe had no alternative but to rely on Mizuno, then serving as a commissioner of naval affairs, who seemed to know much more about the currency question than Manabe himself.

But just when Manabe needed him most, Mizuno was blamed by Ii for the flap over the murder of the foreigners and demoted to post of *Nishi no Maru Rusui*—Caretaker of the West Keep of the Tycoon's palace.

The post was a sinecure that required no work and was usually a last, brief stop for government bureaucrats just before their retirement. It was a position at the fringes of the fringes of power.

The one most upset by Mizuno's exile was Manabe. He opposed Ii's treatment of his favorite, upon whom he depended. Ii, however, held his ground and refused to listen to Manabe's pleas. Mizuno became *Nishi no Maru Rusui* on November 22, eleven days after the burning of the palace. With that, Manabe, who had been Ii's loyal follower, turned his back on the Tairo. He was prepared to resign forthwith.

Since assuming power, Ii had replaced one minister and bureaucrat after another. Given Manabe's attitude, Ii was prepared to dismiss one or two of his troublesome subordinate's people at any time.

Faced with these problems, Manabe had neglected to reply to Alcock's letter. But the British minister was doggedly persistent. So Manabe, thinking to leave everything up to the vice ministers, finally sent a reply asking Alcock to meet with them. Now Alcock's latest letter had arrived, demanding that Japan choose either war or peace.

The Tycoon's ministers took Alcock's threats extremely seriously. They knew how fearsome the British could be. The Opium War and the more recent Arrow War had made them aware, however dimly, of British power. Fear of the unknown is stronger than fear of the known. And now the diplomatic representative of these terrible English was asking them whether they wanted war or peace. They had no choice but to accept his demands. Ii and Manabe compromised. Two days after receiving Alcock's letter, which seemed to be handing them an ultimatum, Manabe and Wakisaka went to see the British minister.

※

Alcock had ceased to trouble himself about the irritating "instructions." He was in no mood to trade pleasantries with his visitors. He began the meeting without preliminaries:

"I am a representative of the British government. I do not possess any ships of war, but I am sure you are well aware of

British military power, and British naval power in particular. I would like you to keep that power in mind as you listen to what I have to say.

"We can settle our differences in two ways. One is to discuss them peacefully. The other is to commence hostilities. England does not like to fight, but given your attitude, we may have to go to war. It all depends on whether or not you wish to observe the treaty. What is your answer, gentlemen?"

Alcock was forcing the issue. Manabe capitulated completely. After this, though he did not acquiesce to each and every one of Alcock's demands, he was much more willing to listen to—and accept them—than he had been before. He quickly agreed to resume the exchange of ichibus on the same basis as before.

Having finished discussing the business at hand, Alcock added, "What I have said today is upon my own authority. However, the representatives of America and France share my sentiments exactly. I urge you to comply with our request. Otherwise, we will present a note signed jointly by the three powers—Great Britain, the United States, and France."

Alcock was giving them an ultimatum. If the Bakufu did not respond by the deadline set by the three powers, they would issue a declaration of war. He continued, saying, "As I mentioned earlier, ships carrying the ministers of Great Britain and France, who were on their way to North China to exchange ratifications for the Treaty of Tientsin, were treacherously fired upon by the Chinese government forts and as you have no doubt heard, suffered a crushing defeat in the resulting battle."

Alcock had feared that, on learning of this attack, the Japanese government might regard Great Britain with contempt and consequently feel free to impose various barriers, beginning with restrictions on commerce.

"My country, however, has no intention of withdrawing from China because of this setback. Within four or five months a fleet of warships will be sent from my country and, joining hands with the French, will bring about the fall of Peking. I would like to you to be aware of our intentions."

Alcock had spoken the truth: a joint Anglo-French force was on its way to attack Peking.

"I hope and pray that our relations with Japan will not come to that pass."

Alcock then returned to a discussion of China:

"Although we concluded the Treaty of Nanking and entered into diplomatic relations with China more than twenty years ago, the Chinese government has consistently defied the treaty. This defiance was the cause of the Arrow War, which ended last year. We then concluded a new treaty—the Treaty of Tientsin—and the British minister left for Peking to exchange ratifications. The minister and his party were nefariously attacked, precipitating the current conflict. It goes without saying that this conflict began because the Chinese government violated the treaty."

Staring intently at his visitors, Alcock fired this parting shot: "If treaties are to be broken, it is best not to make them in the first place."

Japan had not signed the treaty of its own free will—it had been pressured into signing. Listening to Alcock's threatening words, the junior officials at the ministry of foreign affairs who had accompanied their superiors to this meeting gritted their teeth in anger and frustration.

✳

There was one thing, however, that Alcock could not understand. He and Harris had advised the Japanese government to raise the value of the cobang before the Yokohama gold rush started in earnest. If the Japanese had followed their advice, they could have stopped the outflow of cobangs. Instead, they had responded with ridiculous excuses and had done nothing to increase the value of gold. Nothing had changed at all. The day that Alcock issued this threat to Manabe, he shook his head with wonder and dismay.

Soon after coming to Japan he had told the Japanese that if they did not raise the value of cobangs when the exchange of ichibus began, the gold coins would flow out of the country. But instead they had done nothing. What on earth were they think-ing?

That was not the only thing puzzling Alcock: he could also not understand why the Japanese had such an aversion to the dollar.

Their reluctance to accept the dollar, which had never altered, had been the original barrier to trade. If the Japanese had only accepted the dollar in trade, it would not have been necessary to change it for ichibus.

Initially, Alcock had thought that the Japanese rejected the dollar because the Tycoon's government, seemingly the domi-nant power in domestic politics, was compelling them to do so. For a short period immediately after the opening of the ports that kind of coercion may have been possible. But now that five months had passed since the beginning of trade, Alcock had to discard that theory—and wonder what the real problem was. Now the Bakufu was melting down dollars and reminting them as ichibus. Ichibus and dollars were both silver—and silver was silver. But the Japanese continued to shun the dollar and refused to accept it. Alcock could not understand.

Soon after issuing his threat to Manabe, Alcock met with Harris and Bellecourt. He described his meeting with the Japa-nese in detail and freely expressed his doubts concerning the currency question.

Like Alcock, Harris could not understand why the Japanese government did not raise the value of gold. He reasoned that the Japanese must be prejudiced against the dollar because it was not engraved with their government's stamp.

"When I meet them this time, I will propose that, instead of reminting dollars into ichibus, they can save time and trouble by simply engraving the dollar to indicate that it is worth three ichibus. If they do that, anyone would be able to use dollars anywhere in the country. The Japanese will have their official guarantee written on each coin."

Following this discussion with Alcock, Harris met with a minister of foreign affairs on December 25.

By this time, the relationship between Ii and Manabe was

approaching a crisis. Pleading illness, Manabe confined himself indoors. Suspicious of his subordinate's intentions, Ii had Manabe's every movement shadowed.

Harris visited Wakisaka, the other minister of foreign affairs, at his official residence, near the Tycoon's palace.

After enumerating his complaints, Harris said, "Cobangs are flowing out of the country because the cobang's value in relation to the ichibu is extremely low. If you were to triple the value of the cobang, you would make the ratio of gold to silver in Japan the same as that current in the rest of the world and cobangs would no longer leave the country. I strongly advise you to do this."

He then added, "I have spoken of this before, but if the government exchange houses in Yokohama, Nagasaki, and Hakodate were to engrave the dollar to indicate that it is worth three ichibus, Japanese could also use it. I urge you to do this as well."

Wakisaka listened intently to Harris's suggestions.

Three days after Harris's visit to the official residence, Bellecourt also met with Wakisaka. Well aware that his knowledge of the currency question was slight, Bellecourt directed Wakisaka's attention to other matters. Harris went to the official residence again the day after Bellecourt's visit.

Wakisaka first spoke at length about various problems related to engraving the dollar to pass for three ichibus, but added that, in general, he agreed with Harris's suggestion. He did not come out in favor of raising the value of gold, saying that "there are still various matters we wish to study." The Bakufu, he said, had decided to issue dollars engraved with the government stamp so that they could pass for three ichibus.

In mid-January 1860, following Harris's suggestion, the Bakufu began issuing dollars engraved with the characters for *sanbu tsuyo* to indicate that they were equivalent to three ichibus.

Sometimes economic actions lead to unexpected consequences—and illuminate the psychology of those affected. The Japanese who first saw the dollars engraved with *sanbu tsuyo* (good for three ichibus) wondered what they were supposed to be. They finally decided that they were the same as dollars. " 'Good for three ichibus'? Who are they trying to fool?" they said, laughing. They began to refuse to accept the engraved dollars.

But these "three ichibu" dollars were more than a joke: they were a nuisance. Because they would be punished by the authorities if they did not honor them for the amount engraved, people came to refuse them even more firmly. Finally the dollar disappeared from the marketplace altogether.

On February 11, about one month after first issuing the engraved dollars, the Bakufu announced that it would raise the value of the cobang 3.375 times, beginning in ten days, on February 21. It had been six months since Harris had first recommended that the cobang's value be increased.

Alcock settled himself, his writing implements arrayed before him on his desk, to an evening of personal correspondence. The issues that tormented him could neither be discussed with the elderly female relations at home with whom he maintained a polite if irregular exchange of letters, nor could he confide completely in the one man who should have been his closest ally: Townsend Harris. Alcock was still undecided about the American's motives. He chose to pour out his frustrations in a letter to a diplomatic colleague still serving on the China coast.

He wrote frankly of his successes and disappointments in his new post. On the one hand, there were a number of humiliating failures, such as the blow of having Yokohama chosen over Kanagawa as the open treaty port, thereby ensuring that the foreign community would remain in a state of near-quarantine from all but a tiny minority of the Japanese population. He likened it to the Chinese attempt to keep foreigners outside the walls of their cities. This had come about through an unwitting collaboration between the Japanese authorities and the foreign merchants, whose concerns strayed little from their account ledgers, he recorded, with a twinge of disgust.

Then there was the thoroughly unsuccessful attempt to issue a dollar with its value in ichibus stamped on it in Japanese. What possessed these people, wrote Alcock, his blood pressure rising as he wrote with increasing fury, to reject the dollar time and again, when they admit it's perfectly good silver coinage? What more do they want? "Pure, unalloyed perverseness," he fumed.

On the other hand, he could not regard the recent decision of the

Bakufu to devalue their gold piece, the cobang, in conformance with the world standard, as other than a feather in his diplomatic cap. That would end cobang profiteering once and for all, he congratulated himself (he was unaware, of course, that it had ended a month earlier because of an increase in the price of cobangs naturally caused by the boom). He was certain that Harris—at his urging—had done the Japanese a great favor by persuading them to alter the parity of their gold and silver. For all the apparent sophistication of certain aspects of their culture, the Japanese were rather childlike in many ways, he felt. At least in this instance, he had followed Her Majesty's instructions and acted in a friendly fashion toward Japan.

Alcock put down his pen. That last was not quite the whole of the truth. There was the small matter of his having threatened war. But Alcock decided not to mention that. Even in a casual letter to an old friend, frankness had its limits.

5

Discovery

The supreme ruler of Japan was the Tycoon or, as the Japanese usually called him, the Shogun.

The Tycoon, however, was only one *daimyo*, or feudal lord, whose rule extended over no more than one-seventh of the country. His political power was formally delegated to him by the mikado—the emperor—who lived in Japan's former capital, Kyoto. He was thus an unusual "supreme ruler," indeed. The closest European equivalent to Shogun would be "generalissimo." But in their dealings with the outside world, the Japanese usually referred to the Shogun as the Taikun (Tycoon), a seldom-used title that means great sovereign. *Tycoon* would later, of course, become an American colloquialism for "big businessman."

Although the Bakufu—the Tycoon's government—represented Japan as a whole, it should really be called a shogunal, rather than a national, government. It thus had a character somewhat different from that of European governments.

The nucleus of the shogunal government was the Council of State, whose ministers were called Roju. This council was subordinate to the Shogun, the titular sovereign of the country. As a general rule, the prime minister was the most senior Roju.

The Roju were midlevel *daimyo*. Few were qualified other than by birth for their posts, and many were incompetent.

In times of crisis, a Tairo, or regent, temporarily took over the reins of government. This post was filled by a great feudal lord who was a member of a select group of noble families.

Since the middle of the Tokugawa shogunate, which lasted nearly 250 years, the post of Tairo had been merely decorative and honorary. Even so, officially the Tairo ranked above the Roju and presided over them.

Since the signing of the treaties, the Tairo had been Ii Naosuke, the Prince of Hikone, an arch-conservative. But Ii had been an exceptional Tairo—instead of being a figurehead, he had wielded absolute power.

On March 24, 1860—one month after the government raised the value of the cobang to the world gold standard—Ii was attacked and beheaded by a band of ten unidentified assassins as he was on his way to the Tycoon's palace. The assassins had ambushed him just outside the palace's Sakuradamon Gate.

This murder of a Tairo in broad daylight, in sight of his own home (the Ii mansion in Miyazaka), and in front of a bridge that passed over to the Tycoon's palace, greatly shocked Alcock, Harris, and the other foreign diplomats.

Alcock was unaware of the distinction between a Roju and a Tairo. Also, he and the other diplomats did not know that Ii, who had held supreme power, had ruled by terror and harshly suppressed his opponents. Although they gathered information from various sources about Ii's assassination, they did not pay close attention to his political stance or changes in the political situation that might result from his death. This was testimony to the effectiveness with which Ii had managed information, using secret police methods.

After Ii's assassination, Kuze Hirochika, the Prince of Seki-yado, and Ando Nobumasa, the Prince of Iwaki, seized power.

Ando had been a member of Ii's Council of State, winning a promotion from Wakadoshiyori—vice minister—to Roju. He had also served as minister of foreign affairs. At the time of his ascension, however, he was still a newcomer to the council. To enhance his authority and eradicate all traces of Ii's rule, he welcomed Kuze into the council, and together they formed a coalition government. Kuze had been a member of the council for many years, but had clashed with Ii and resigned.

The political line adopted by the Kuze-Ando administration differed from Ii's. They aimed to repair the strained relationship between the Bakufu and the mikado and placate public opinion.

The mikado, Emperor Komei, was a rabid exclusionist. The word *joi* (which means "expel the barbarian") had become a popular rallying cry of the time. The "barbarians" were the Europeans. Emperor Komei was a leading symbol of the *joi* movement.

Ii, an ultra-conservative, had had a strong ideological affinity with the exclusionist cause. He thus did not welcome the arrival of Harris, Alcock, and the other foreign representatives.

Soon after being appointed Tairo, however, Ii had impulsively agreed to permit the signing of the commercial treaty the previous prime minister, Hotta Masayoshi, had negotiated with Harris. He thus reluctantly took his stand with the progressives, who were for the opening of the country, and suppressed the *joi* forces.

Ii was a stubborn, willful man. He brought such unwarranted severe pressure to bear on his opponents—pressure for the sake of pressure—that public opinion turned completely against him. The antagonism he aroused finally led to his assassination. Inevitably, in spite of the ideological common ground between the two men, some of those who had been crushed by Ii had had connections with Emperor Komei.

The emperor had been a politically impotent figure almost since the earliest recorded history. But in the confusion surrounding the opening of the country, Emperor Komei discovered his latent political strength.

He could not, however, easily display this strength during Ii's reign of terror. Then Ii was felled by an assassin's sword, and the mikado bounded out of his restrictive nominal role. No longer able to ignore his influence, the Kuze-Ando administration tried to mend ties with him.

Ever since the Ii administration, there had been talk of marrying Kazunomiya, the mikado's younger sister, to Shogun Iemochi. Hoping to improve relations with the emperor, the

Kuze-Ando government tried to play matchmaker. They eagerly appealed to Kyoto to let Kazunomiya become Iemochi's consort.

In his brief reply to this appeal, Emperor Komei twice referred to "expelling the barbarians." The Bakufu interpreted this to mean that if it took decisive action to expel the barbarians, the emperor would permit the marriage. Emperor Komei, a hard-line *joi* advocate, had doubtless intended to imply as much in his letter. Kuze and Ando leaped at the suggestion.

It was not in the power of the Bakufu, however, to expel the barbarian. Instead, it proposed postponing the opening of Hyogo and Niigata to trade and Edo and Osaka to foreign settlement. By deferring the quickly approaching opening of these ports and cities, which had been stipulated in the commercial treaties signed with five nations, they could demonstrate their intention to expel the barbarian. The diplomatic problem of asking the treaty nations to delay the opening of the ports and cities had thus become entangled with domestic politics. Ando, the minister of foreign affairs, approached Alcock and Harris about agreeing to a postponement.

The minister plenipotentiary of Prussia, Count Friedrich Albert Eulenburg, came to Japan in September with special orders to "conclude a commercial treaty with Japan." The Bakufu, however, was in the midst of negotiating a delay in the opening of the two ports and two cities with the foreign representatives. Ando refused Eulenburg's request to negotiate a commercial treaty, saying, "we cannot sign a new treaty under any conditions."

✳

Harris was a sociable man. But he looked down upon and remained standoffish toward the American merchants living in Yokohama. Harris could unburden himself only to his diplomatic colleagues in Edo or the naval officers of various nationalities who occasionally came to visit him.

Not surprisingly, the Americans living in Yokohama were strongly prejudiced against Harris for what they saw as his "haughtiness and airs." Three missionary families in Kanagawa, however, were different.

The missionary families were staying at Jobutsuji Temple— a fact that reflected the lack of religious dogmatism in Japanese Buddhism. Luckily for Harris, the temple was only a seven- or eight-minute walk from the American consulate. One family was that of James Curtis Hepburn, who later became known for his Hepburn System of romanizing Japanese.

Another was that of S. R. Brown, his wife, and their two young daughters. At this time there were only twelve European women in Yokohoma and Kanagawa. Five—the three missionary wives and the two Hepburn girls—were living at Jobutsuji. The temple thus had a certain sparkle and charm for the many male callers who visited there frequently, even though they had no pressing business.

Harris considered himself a devout Episcopalian and generally behaved as such. The Hepburns and the other two families had come to Japan to spread the message of Christ. To Harris, they were of a different order from the American merchants in Yokohama. Also, unlike the merchants, the missionary families lived in Kanagawa, which he and other diplomats had demanded be made an open port. Although the missionaries had settled in Kanagawa because they felt that there they would have more opportunities to meet and proselytize the Japanese, their choice was a welcome one for Harris. Also, the three wives and two young ladies added considerable spice to his social life. Harris's demeanor changed completely when he visited the three families. He played the good-natured uncle who never failed to bring unusual presents from Edo.

The three families at Jobutsuji responded in kind: they alone among the foreigners greeted Harris warmly and treated him as a friend.

In New York, where Harris had grown up, people exchanged visits on New Year's Day to celebrate the beginning of another year, just like the Japanese. In Edo, Harris had only familiar faces from which to choose. Visiting the Japanese was not an option. There were, however, the three families at Jobutsuji who welcomed his company. As 1860 drew to a close, Harris left for Kanagawa to celebrate New Year's Day with them.

On New Year's Eve, Harris received a visit from a governor of foreign affairs, who had come from Edo expressly to see him, bearing yet another tale of a certain Mito no Goroko.

Mito no Goroko—Mito the Old Nobleman—was a name often mentioned by the Japanese. Mito was a catchall scapegoat, invariably blamed (whether correctly or not, no one ever knew for certain) for anything that went wrong, until the foreign diplomats tired of hearing about him. The assassin who had beheaded the Tairo Ii was rumored to be a former retainer of Mito no Goroko. The governor of foreign affairs had called on Harris this New Year's Eve to tell him that the Roju had definite information that several hundred *ronin*—samurai formerly re- tained by none other than the infamous Mito no Goroko—had assembled in two groups: one to set fire to foreign residences in Yokohama, the other to attack the diplomatic legations in Edo and to kill the foreigners employed there.

"Until we can arrest these men and end this disturbance, it would be best for you and the other foreign representatives to leave your legations temporarily and evacuate to a building inside the moat of the Tycoon's palace. Also, please instruct your consular representatives to move to Yokohama so that we can better protect them."

Not again, thought Harris in disgust. This was a transparent ploy to shut up the diplomatic representatives in the Tycoon's palace and herd the consuls into Yokohama.

"You will not be able to use such a flimsy ruse with me," said Harris in firmly refusing the governor's request. He dismissed him without another word.

But, in any event, he would have to inform his colleagues.

In East Asian countries such as China and Japan, western diplomats were well aware that they had to act in concert. Otherwise, it would be extremely difficult to conduct diplomatic negotiations. When western diplomats failed to present the appearance of unity, Asians were quick to take advantage.

This was regarded as common sense among western diplomats in China and Japan. Harris and Alcock were both well aware of it. In dealing with various matters, including the currency question, they fought on a common front.

Harris, as the senior diplomatic representative in Japan, had a duty to convey the Bakufu's warning to Alcock, Bellecourt, and Eulenburg, of Prussia, with whom he had become intimate over the past four months. Tomorrow, however, was New Year's Day, a day he had planned to spend visiting the three families in Jobutsuji. He was already in Kanagawa and had no intention of returning to Edo. Instead, he wrote letters to his three colleagues. The next day, on the morning of January 1, 1861, Henry C. J. Heusken, Harris's secretary and translator, carried them back to Edo.

※

After spending a pleasant New Year's Day socializing in Kanagawa, Harris returned to Edo. Arriving at the legation, he was greeted by the sight of a cannon that had been brought in by the Japanese government and unceremoniously deposited inside. Supposedly, its purpose was to protect the legation from attackers, but to Harris it smacked of theatricalism.

Harris immediately summoned Alcock, Bellecourt, and Eulenburg. "It's nothing but a ploy," he said disdainfully, showing his visitors the cannon. "That's all it is. They mean to shut us up inside the Tycoon's palace and drive the consuls into Yokohama. I told the Japanese in no uncertain terms that they would not be able to get away with it."

Escorting his visitors back inside the legation, Harris continued to vent his annoyance. "Three years ago, when I first came to Edo to negotiate a commercial treaty, I was warned nearly every day that my life was in danger. A heavy guard was placed around my lodgings and even ordered to patrol at night. This was intended to frighten me and send me packing from Edo. But when the government realized that none of this had any effect on me, they quietly stopped the patrols and withdrew the guard."

The Bakufu had placed a guard around Harris's lodgings

because *ronin* from the Mito clan had shown signs of wanting to attack him. Harris, however, suspected that the Bakufu was using this threat to drive him from Edo. But when he came to know Hotta Masayoshi, the minister of foreign affairs, Harris realized that he was not a man to trifle with such schemes, and his suspicions had been allayed. His colleagues, however, did not know that. Taking advantage of their ignorance, Harris referred to this incident to advance his own case.

Alcock had often heard Harris tell this story. Recently, he had started to wonder whether Harris's version of it might be an exaggeration or, to put it more plainly, a deliberate misrepresentation. He also suspected that Harris might be hiding the truth about his buying of cobangs as well. His story was a little too perfect. Furthermore, Alcock could not believe that the warning was just a Japanese ploy.

"Pardon me, but my view of the situation is slightly different," said Alcock, interrupting. On the evening of January 1, the day he had received Harris's letter, Alcock had had a visit from a governor of foreign affairs concerning the same matter.

"The governor looked at me very gravely—I could detect no deception in his glance. He expressed grave concern about our safety. I do not believe that this is merely a Japanese trick."

Alcock had recently been promoted to minister. The British diplomatic mission was now housed in a legation, and Alcock had carefully observed the Japanese who came there.

"The behavior of the officials and servants betrays fear. Even when the regent was murdered, they did not look so clearly afraid or anxious for their own safety as they do now. We cannot easily determine the truth or falsity of the information we have been provided, but there are definite signs of danger that have given the Japanese government cause for concern. Therefore, I have sent a letter to Rear Admiral Jones in Yokohama requesting that he station two ships in Edo Bay."

As Alcock had already informed the Japanese in October of the previous year, the Anglo-French forces that had been dispatched again to the China coast had fallen on Peking without mercy and quickly captured it. The allied army had come to

Yokohama and Edo to spend the Christmas and New Year's holidays. The day he had received the warning from a governor of foreign affairs, Alcock, deeply concerned about the situation, had sent a letter to Rear Admiral Jones, who had just come from Edo to Yokohama, requesting that he leave two ships behind in Edo Bay.

Until recently, Alcock had not had even one man-of-war at his disposal. But now that the dispute with the Chinese government in Peking had been settled, the rear admiral had granted Alcock's request and left two ships in Edo: the small sloop *Pioneer* and the corvette *Encounter.*

Because the views of Harris and Alcock differed, the foreign diplomats gathered that day at the American legation did not decide to oppose the Japanese government, and the meeting ended inconclusively.

✳

After reaching a compromise, the Bakufu and the Prussian minister had finally agreed to conclude a commercial treaty. On January 15, in a ceremony at the foreigners guest house and Prussian mission in Akabanebashi, Eulenburg presented the Japanese with gifts from the Prussian government to celebrate the imminent signing of the treaty. Henry Heusken, Harris's secretary and a veteran interpreter, had assisted with the negotiations from the beginning. Heusken had been at work from morning until night on this day as well because the Bakufu had requested some minor changes in the wording of the treaty. At about eight-thirty, as he was strolling back to the legation after dinner at the foreigners guest house, Heusken was attacked near Azabu Nakanobashi.

Although Heusken had been accompanied by three mounted officers and four foot soldiers carrying lanterns, when the half-dozen or so attackers pounced, his Japanese guards fled, scattering in all directions.

Finding Heusken groaning in the street, servants from the legation placed him on a board and carried him back to the

legation at around nine o'clock. Harris immediately sent word
to Eulenburg and Alcock and summoned a surgeon.

Alcock had once been a surgeon himself, but had not
practiced for many years. Fortunately, Dr. Myburgh, a medical
officer who also served as a Dutch interpreter, was attached to
the British legation. Alcock sent him to Harris.

Wondering whether the wound would prove fatal, Alcock
spent the night pacing in his quarters.

The two Russians were the first to be killed, thought Alcock.
This is the fifth such incident. The sixth counting Dan, that
heedless but charming Japanese boy.

Alcock's mind wandered from Heusken's condition to the
fate of his former interpreter.

Dan, a Japanese castaway who had learned English from his
rescuers, was a stoker on the *Mississippi* when he heard that the
British consul in Canton had been promoted to the post of
consul general of Japan. Talking his way into the Canton legation, Dan became Alcock's interpreter and messenger and returned with him to Japan. Dan had a naturally violent temper.
During his vagabond days, when he had had to rely on his own
wits and strength to survive, that temper had become even more
violent. Used to independence, Dan had thrown off the yoke of
the Japanese feudal system. He rode into Japan proudly, ready
to hurl himself bodily at the old order and ridicule his countrymen, who were still bound to it.

Fortunately for him, he was an employee of the British
legation. Because of his position, the Japanese could not touch
him. Well aware of their helplessness, Dan began to provoke
them publicly. Japanese could not ride horseback in Edo unless
they were samurai. But even though he had been a mere sailor—
a low rung on the Japanese social ladder—Dan rode horseback
and cracking his whip, habitually raced his mount at a gallop
through the streets.

The samurai that he passed were incensed by Dan's behavior. Dan lashed out at them as though he were baiting them.
More than once, he found himself involved in a quarrel. Several
times, these street rows had come to the attention of the city

magistrate's office, which had judicial as well as police powers. The city magistrate, however, had no judicial authority over Dan and was unable to take any action.

Dan's insolent behavior was notorious among the Edo samurai. More than one had designs on his life. Given the chance, they would have cut him down without hesitation. Alcock was secretly warned of this by the Japanese. He seriously thought of sending Dan abroad for his own protection, but when Alcock broached the idea, Dan refused to listen.

Soon afterward, Dan was stabbed in the back in broad daylight while leaning against the entrance to the legation. Seeing him staggering, with a short sword buried to the hilt in his back, the porter came running. When he drew out the sword, Dan fell face forward, blood spraying from his wound. The point of the sword had hit its mark, piercing his heart.

Alcock was roused from his musings by the sound of hooves and a horse neighing near the legation gate. Dr. Myburgh had returned. Alcock went out to meet him.

"How is he?"

"The moment I saw the wound, I realized that Mr. Heusken's condition was hopeless," replied the doctor.

"And the cut?" asked Alcock, reflexively.

"The cut extended diagonally from the area of the navel across nearly the entire pelvic region. The bowels were protruding, and some of the intestines had been nearly cut through. I did everything I could, but to no avail. Mr. Heusken breathed his last at half an hour past midnight."

"And Mr. Harris?"

"He was weeping at Heusken's side."

That was only to be expected. Harris had lost a close friend and loyal subordinate who had stood by him since Shimoda. Alcock said nothing, but the thought of Harris's loss was uppermost in his mind.

✳

Heusken's funeral was held on January 18. On that day, Alcock passed along the familiar road to the American legation. Arriving, he found the legation surrounded by a mob of curious onlookers. Pushing through the crowd, Alcock entered the gates.

Bellecourt had already arrived. Eulenburg had not yet appeared, but J. K. de Wit, the Dutch consul general, had come from Nagasaki aboard the warship *Cachelot* and hastened to the legation together with the crew.

When Alcock had finished offering his condolences, the Japanese mourners—five governors of foreign affairs—cleared a path through the crowd and entered the legation. One of them expressed his government's regrets to Harris. He then said something so strange that Alcock wondered what the man was thinking of:

"We have received definite word that a band of assassins is coming to attack the funeral procession. The government has taken measures to ensure your safety, but cannot guarantee it. Therefore, we ask you to bury the coffin quietly, with no one accompanying it. We also request that the ministers and their companions stay in their homes."

Preventing such attacks was the Japanese government's sworn duty. And now they had the impudence to suggest that the funeral be called off! Such were the thoughts of the diplomats as they looked at Harris. Conscious that all eyes were upon him, Harris, raising his voice to reply, so that even the crowd outside could hear him, said, "My colleagues and I must perform our duty of love and accompany our murdered friend's body to its final resting place. If the Japanese government has neither the ability nor the will to stop such an attack, we will take measures to protect ourselves."

Having said this, Harris sent a Japanese messenger to Eulenburg, who had not yet arrived, requesting a larger military escort.

Although Harris had raised his voice in replying to the Japanese request, it was a voice that did not have its usual sharpness, spirit, or force.

He has just lost his friend and is exhausted from lack of

sleep, mused Alcock. This struck him as entirely natural and he gave it no further thought.

A grave had been prepared at Korinji Temple, which was about one kilometer from the American legation, in Zenpukuji Temple. The funeral procession departed at one-thirty.

In addition to the ministers, legation staff members, and Yokohama consuls, the procession included Prussian and Dutch officers and seamen, who were guarding the diplomats, and the naval band from the *Arcona*, a Prussian warship. The procession was headed by the five governors of foreign affairs on horseback.

Alcock had armed himself with a pistol and short sword. The military escort shouldered rifles loaded with live ammunition as they moved forward to guard the route.

The procession came to a stream running along the left side of the road. There were ample places from which to launch an ambush, such as the bridges that spanned the stream, the street corners, where visibility was poor, and the hedges to their right. The procession moved forward with caution.

The Japanese governors of foreign affairs, who were leading the procession, warned that there was danger of an attack. "We have taken precautions for your safety," they said. But the mourners could detect no signs of Japanese bodyguards.

"I don't see that a single soldier has been summoned," said one.

"And not only that," said another, "they have taken no measures to guard against a surprise attack on the road."

"The story about a gang coming to attack us is a complete fiction. They merely wanted to threaten us so that we wouldn't join the procession."

The diplomats vented their contempt for the governors' all-too-transparent lies.

The procession arrived at Korinji. A deep hole had been dug at Heusken's grave site. Next to it was the grave of Dan, marked by a plain wooden post.

The coffin was lowered into the grave. A priest, who was also a translator attached to the French legation, conducted the service according to the Catholic liturgy. The military band played a mournful hymn, a soldier dipped the American flag, and each of the bareheaded mourners tossed a handful of earth into the grave. Then a Buddhist priest who had been dispatched by the Bakufu recited sutras.

The ceremony ended peacefully. Harris thanked the mourners in a brief but emotional speech. They then filed silently out of the cemetery.

"Would everyone please give me their attention for a moment?" Alcock called to his colleagues when they had passed through the gates of Korinji.

"If the Japanese had good reason to know that there was danger, they were bound by every motive of national good faith and honor to strain the utmost powers of the government to avert it and afford protection. If no such danger existed and they issued the warning simply to keep us from joining the procession, it is an infamy and outrage. I would like to meet with you to discuss the situation we now find ourselves in, as well as what measures we should take to protect our personal safety, our national honor, and the lives and fortunes of all foreigners in Japan."

Everyone agreed with this proposal. The next day, the ministers gathered at the British legation to discuss what should be done. Word of this meeting was also conveyed to Harris, who had remained behind at the cemetery.

✳

"By now there have been many cases of foreigners murdered—many victims have fallen at the hands of assassins."

"The Japanese government has yet to capture even one criminal. I wonder how hard they are trying."

It was with these comments, emerging unprompted from the lips of the participants, that the day's meeting began.

De Wit, the Dutch consul general from Nagasaki, was not well acquainted with the situation in Edo; he attended as an observer. Because Prussia had not yet signed a commercial treaty with Japan, Eulenburg, the Prussian minister, had also originally been an observer at these meetings, but he had now been in Edo four months and was an active participant in the discussion. Bellecourt, of France, who had just been promoted to the rank of minister, tended to follow the lead of Alcock and Harris and not assert his own views. He did not speak as much as the others. The leader of the meeting was Alcock. Harris, who was usually highly conscious of his position as senior diplomat and spoke as though he were in contention with Alcock, the representative of a Great Power, was oddly quiet today.

He has just lost Heusken. It's only natural that he be in low spirits, thought Alcock as he began the meeting.

"Further protests are useless—a waste of time and effort. Nothing we say to the Japanese will change or improve the situation. It will simply become more chaotic and confused. Also, our lives will continue to be threatened indiscriminately. I therefore propose that we withdraw our legations from Edo temporarily and move them to Yokohama. There we can receive adequate protection from two British ships of war. Furthermore, our removal to Yokohama in itself will place great pressure on the Japanese government."

Nearly everyone agreed with Alcock's proposal. Just one shook his head in disagreement: Mr. Harris. He finally broke his silence, saying, "The Japanese government has consistently warned the diplomatic representatives of the existing dangers from the first day of their arrival in this city and has shown its anxiety to secure their safety.

"We have been in Edo for nineteen months in safety, and this fact is proof of the desire and ability of the government to give us effective protection."

Harris ordinarily had nothing good to say about the Bakufu. Only two weeks before, he had been extremely caustic in describing the Bakufu's warning as a "ploy." Now he was extolling the Bakufu's sincerity and good faith. Alcock was not the only one astonished by this turnabout.

"I know that everyone regrets the loss of Mr. Heusken, who was a loyal and able interpreter at the American legation. His loss is particularly painful to me. But we must all remember that this tragedy occurred because Mr. Heusken disregarded the reiterated warnings of the Japanese government against his constant exposure of himself at night."

Harris, who had previously maintained that "diplomats in the East have to harmonize their views and act as one" was now ignoring the diplomatic common sense that he himself had been the first to practice—Harris, the senior diplomat, the one with the most experience in Japan. Alcock could not believe his own eyes and ears.

Harris was an eloquent speaker. His words flowed smoothly and rapidly, betraying no hint of awareness that he was reversing his earlier position.

"To return to Yokohama with the intention of producing an effect on the Japanese government will, I think, prove a mistake—that is exactly what they want. There was no article in the American treaty more difficult to obtain than the one securing a residence in Edo for the diplomatic representative of the United States. The Japanese governors on that occasion warned me of the grave difficulties such a residence in Edo would cause and they were very solicitous that I should accept a permanent residence in Kanagawa or Kawasaki with the right to come to Edo whenever duty required."

Initially, Iwase, the chief Japanese negotiator, had made such a request. But he had quickly retreated and substituted the condition that the minister's arrival at his post be delayed by a year and a half. Alcock and the others, however, did not know that. Once again, Harris had distorted the facts to suit his own convenience.

"The retirement of the foreign legations to Yokohama is exactly what the government desires, as it relieves them from great anxiety, responsibility, and expense. They state that the legations can be more conveniently protected at Yokohama than in Edo. Therefore, instead of the retirement giving a swipe to the Japanese government, they will view it as highly desirable. I apprehend that a residence in Yokohama will further encourage the Japanese mind to confound the foreign representatives with the foreign traders, an effect that cannot fail to injure both our prestige and our influence."

As his senior colleague's monologue showed no signs of ending, Alcock interrupted. "Just a moment please, Mr. Harris. Until now we have discussed the necessity of making the Japanese government amend its neglect. If we do as you say, we will in effect be accepting that neglect."

"That may be so," replied Harris, "but I say that we have to trust the sincerity of the Japanese government and see how the situation develops, for at least a little while longer. Retiring to Yokohama now would be a tactical blunder."

"But in our previous discussions, you consistently denied that the Japanese government had ever demonstrated sincerity or good faith."

"Not 'ever,' Mr. Alcock. If you review the history of the past nineteen months, I think you will find ample cause to trust in the Japanese government's sincerity and good faith."

The discussion was beginning to sound more like an argument. Eulenburg intervened, saying, "In view of the circumstances, I believe that the decision of the British, French, and Dutch ministers is correct. But because the current situation does not absolutely demand united action, the American minister should be allowed to act as he thinks best. Mr. Harris was the first to conclude a commercial treaty with Japan and has lived in Japan longer than the rest of us. He has his own view of the matter, and even if he remains behind, it will not in any way harm the interests of the representatives who remove to Yokohama. In fact, his presence here might serve to calm those disturbances, which concern us all."

Actually, Harris's presence in Edo could seriously harm the interests of the other foreign representatives—specifically, those of Alcock and Bellecourt—but even so, Eulenburg's somewhat inconsistent attempt at peacemaking calmed Alcock and Harris and brought the argument to an end.

Two days later Alcock again called a meeting of foreign representatives. But feeling that Harris would not alter his views and that his presence would only disturb the meeting, Alcock did not issue him an invitation. That day, Alcock and the others decided to withdraw to Yokohama, despite Harris's opposition.

Alcock had the *Encounter* and the *Pioneer*—the two warships in Yokohama—come to the Shinagawa offing. Lending one ship to Bellecourt, Alcock boarded the other with his staff and sailed to Yokohama. The second meeting of foreign representatives was held five days later, on January 26.

Heusken, the secretary and translator, had been the American legation's only staff member. Now Heusken was dead and Harris remained in Edo alone.

✳

Acting Consul Howard Vyse was living in Kanagawa with his wife. Alcock could not very well ask to lodge in a room at the consulate for a long period of time. After arriving in Yokohama, Alcock stayed at the Yokohama Hotel, a new establishment that had a western-style bar and restaurant as well as—a true rarity in Japan—a billiards table.

In the nineteen months since the opening of the ports, Alcock had always acted in concert with Harris. His senior colleague's sudden change of attitude after Heusken's murder had been completely unexpected. Until recently, Alcock and Harris had harmonized their views and coordinated their dealings with the Japanese. Even in their private lives, the two bachelors had gotten along well.

Why has Harris altered his views so suddenly? Has something happened to make him change so? Is he really telling the truth? Sitting in a rocking chair in his hotel room on the Bund, gazing out the window toward Edo on the other side of the water, Alcock spent his days pondering Harris's inexplicable transformation.

Harris, on the other hand, had begun a life of maddening isolation, painfully aware that his colleagues most likely suspected his motives.

The misconduct of the officers and crew on board the *Powhatan*—namely, their frenzied speculation in cobangs—had been reported in the *North China Herald* and described in letters

sent directly to the United States. It did not take long before the
U.S. government became fully apprised.

In addition to buying cobangs, the *Powhatan*'s officers had
used the remaining 60,000 of the original 150,000 ichibus to
purchase goods and charter a merchant ship. Loading the goods
on board, the merchantman had set sail for Hong Kong. The
cargo was large—and troublesome to sell—but the officers finally disposed of it by conducting an auction. The U.S. government had also been informed of this in letters sent from Hong
Kong. When the *Powhatan* returned to Yokohama from Hong
Kong, the officers obtained another 110,000 ichibus, which they
used to buy cobangs. The U.S. government knew this as well.

The Japanese diplomatic mission had boarded the *Powhatan*
and sailed to Panama via Honolulu and San Francisco. At Panama the Japanese disembarked, crossed the isthmus by train and
arriving at the Atlantic, headed for Washington. The Japanese
returned via the Cape of Good Hope aboard the *Niagara*, a ship
dispatched by the U.S. government. The U.S. government had
also given the *Niagara* an official letter for Harris. It stated that
he was to "investigate and report on the misconduct of the
Powhatan's officers and crew."

Harris was well acquainted with the misconduct of the
Powhatan's officers and crew. It was he, after all, who had advised
them to take as many ichibus as possible. Racking his brains to
write something that would divert attention from his part in
the matter, Harris finished his report and sent it. Then came the
New Year. Not long after returning to Edo, Harris received the
order he had been dreading:

"Because it is suspected that you yourself may have been
speculating in Japanese currency, you are hereby relieved of
responsibility for the investigation into the misconduct of the
Powhatan's officers and crew."

After issuing this order to Harris, the U.S. government
organized a committee to conduct an independent investigation.
In the course of that investigation, the committee discovered
that, prior to the opening of the port of Kanagawa (actually,

Yokohama), the American minister had sold a large quantity of cobangs in Shanghai.

In Harris's written records of November 7, 1857—over three years before—he had written, "My outlay is about $1,500 per annum. But . . . I can remit to New York some $6,000 per annum as my savings out of a salary of $5,000!"

What had been Harris's original purpose in coming to Japan? The evidence indicates he had come for no other purpose than to enrich himself.

If his expenses amounted to $1,500 out of a yearly salary of $5,000, he should have been left with $3,500. But Harris was able to remit $6,000 to New York. Somehow, he had managed to save an extra $2,500. How had he done it? Just as Alcock had suspected: by speculation in cobangs.

Soon after arriving in Japan, Harris had learned that the ratio of gold to silver was extremely low—about one to five. Internationally, the ratio was one to sixteen. Like the foreign merchants in Yokohama, Harris soon realized that by having the Japanese agree to a weight-for-weight exchange rate and exchanging ichibus for cobangs at the official rate, he could obtain enormous profits. But if this situation were allowed to continue, Japan's gold—its cobangs—would disappear when the country became fully open. Harris was aware that Alcock wondered why, knowing this, he had done nothing. He also realized that Alcock had two important weaknesses: a tendency to believe too readily what he was told, and a priggish unwillingness to face the unpleasant. Harris therefore was, correctly, able to discount the irascible Englishman as a serious impediment to his designs.

Harris represented himself as a devout Christian and a man of principle. Had he really been either, he would have informed the Japanese that their ratio of gold to silver was low as soon as he knew of it and advised them on ways to keep gold from flowing out of the country. To do so should have been his proper business and responsibility, but Harris did nothing because he was dazzled by the prospect of making a killing that required minimal effort on his part.

Harris's negotiating partners in Shimoda—the local authorities—were easily intimidated. Harris, who had an unerring nose for the weaknesses of others, not only bullied them during the negotiations but later had them collect cobangs and bring them to the legation.

To clear a profit of $2,500, Harris must have obtained nearly 1,000 cobangs. He established his consulate at Gyokusenji Temple in Kakizaki Village, about one and a half kilometers east of Shimoda. His private quarters were in the rear eight-mat room on the left, facing Gyokusenji's main temple building. Looking at this room, which has remained unchanged since Harris's time, it is easy to imagine the bent form of a middle-aged man, counting his cobangs one by one by the light of a candle and muttering, "This will earn me about two thousand five hundred dollars." That would be close to a true picture of Harris.

Between Perry's visit and Harris's arrival, warships and other vessels visited Shimoda several times. Each time they came, they paid for their expenses in gold coins. "Besides," Harris recorded, "I have made a little sum of about $2,500 by taking from the Japanese foreign gold at the rate at which they took it—i.e., 34½ cents per dollar."

Harris had come to Japan with $5,000—his annual salary, paid in advance. When he totaled his personal accounts at the end of the year, he had $3,500 left. He had also earned a $2,500 profit from cobangs and a $2,500 profit from foreign gold, for a total profit of $5,000. He thus ended the year $8,500 in the black.

The U.S. dollar of the 1850s was much stronger than today's. Even at the lowest estimate, it was worth about 300 times its present value. In one year, Harris thus made about $2,500,000 in present-day dollars.

Just after the opening of the ports, there was an incident involving Henry Heusken—Harris's secretary and interpreter abruptly left his post without permission. This incident was also caused by Harris's cobang profiteering.

A young Dutch immigrant to the United States, Heusken had been looking for work in New York when he heard that Harris needed an interpreter. He applied for the job, was hired, and went to Japan. Like Harris, Heusken soon realized that the ratio of gold to silver was low and that he could make a fortune if he bought cobangs.

With the help of Moriyama Takichiro, the Dutch interpreter for the Japanese, who could also understand a little English, Harris was able to obtain cobangs secretly. Learning of this, Heusken asked Moriyama to do the same for him.

Moriyama refused. The local authorities had told him that there was "no need to supply cobangs to the interpreter." Heusken thus had to ask Harris directly. If Harris refused, Heusken would threaten to divulge his secret to the Europeans who would soon be coming to Japan in increasing numbers.

But Heusken found Harris accommodating. "Don't worry, I'll give you your share," Harris replied when Heusken approached him.

Harris secretly took cobangs out of the country when he went to Shanghai aboard the *Mississippi,* which made a timely visit to Japan in April of 1859, just three months prior to the opening of the ports. Heusken, who remained behind at Shimoda, saw Harris off, expecting that he would get a large cut of the profits.

Harris returned from Shanghai on June 26, just prior to the opening of the ports. Heusken watched the servants unload considerably less baggage than they had loaded on for the trip to Shanghai. Heusken naturally assumed that Harris had changed the cobangs as planned, but his boss did not broach the subject of his share.

Boarding the *Mississippi,* Harris and Heusken left Shimoda and arrived at the Kanagawa offing on June 30, the day before the ports were to open to the British. Harris had as yet said nothing. Unable to contain himself, Heusken brought up the subject on the evening of July 3, the day before the ports were to open to the Americans. Harris took out a package he had prepared. It was not nearly as big as Heusken had expected. He refused it and demanded a larger share.

On July 4, American Independence Day, the ports opened to the Americans. That day, Harris, accompanied by Vice-Consul E. M. Dorr and the captain and officers of the *Mississippi*, went ashore at Kanagawa and proceeded to the consulate in Honkakuji Temple, where they celebrated the double holiday. While Harris and the others were ashore, Heusken left the ship and boarded a Dutch merchantman that had just come into port, quitting his job without notice.

When he found Heusken gone, Harris was stunned. If Heusken let it be known that he had been buying cobangs, it would ruin everything. His reputation as a diplomat would be destroyed, and he would be made a laughingstock. Harris presented himself to the world as a devout Christian. Cobang profiteering was one of the most shameful acts a devout Christian could commit, especially one serving as a diplomatic representative.

Harris was desperate; somehow or other he had to get Heusken back, no matter what the cost. The only way to do it, he realized, was to give him a satisfactory share of the profits.

Should he leave the ship and tell this to Heusken himself? He had his reputation as a minister to consider, and if Heusken refused, it would only add to his shame. Instead, he wrote a letter saying that he was willing to pay Heusken an adequate share. Of course, he could not deliver it himself. Should he have a crew member from the *Mississippi* take it? But there was the danger that the messenger might glimpse the contents.

The next day, July 5, the *Mississippi* dropped Harris off at Edo and sailed immediately for the China coast. Harris waited until the ship had departed before entering Edo the following day. Moriyama, the interpreter, was among the officials who greeted him. Harris entrusted him with the letter to Heusken, and Moriyama left for Yokohama by the overland route.

Harris had no guarantee that Heusken would return. Worried that Heusken might refuse his offer and remain at large,

Harris wrote a letter to the State Department and dispatched it with the *Mississippi*.

"I regret to inform you that Mr. Heusken, my Dutch interpreter, left me this afternoon without giving me a single day to provide a substitute.

"I have strong suspicions as to the means that were used to induce Mr. Heusken to act in a manner so contrary to the rules of propriety and integrity, and to leave this legation at a most important juncture, and in a manner so well calculated to embarrass and injure the interests of the United States."

Harris thus became the first to point a finger, by suggesting that Heusken had been buying cobangs.

"But as they are only suspicions, I do not feel warranted in giving you any particulars until what is now suspicion shall become ascertained fact. I cannot obtain an interpreter at once, but I shall use all possible efforts to procure such temporary aid as will prevent injury to our affairs in this country."

Here, also, Harris avoided touching on the substance of his suspicions.

The next day, July 6, Rutherford Alcock had returned to Edo, more determined than ever to deal with the currency question and the Bakufu's attempt to ghettoize the foreign community in Yokohama. Hearing that Alcock was back, Harris went to the British legation that day. He came straight to the point: "I have grave suspicions concerning Mr. Heusken's conduct."

Alcock, however, had no idea what he was talking about. But he did not ask Harris any questions.

"Until I find a successor to Mr. Heusken, I would like you to lend me one of your Dutch interpreters."

When Alcock granted his request, Harris was overjoyed.

Heusken, on the other hand, was satisfied with Harris's letter in which he ceded to the translator's blackmail. He had won the contest of wills—and a fair share of the profits.

He sent Harris a reply saying that he would return to work.

Now Harris had another problem: the nasty letter about Heusken that he had sent to the State Department. The *Missis-*

sippi had already borne it away from Edo. It would not be possible to call it back. Harris dashed off a second letter, saying that it had all been a misunderstanding and that Heusken had left his employment believing that he had Mr. Harris's permission to do so and that he had returned to service the moment he realized that his impressions were wrong. The State Department officials who read both letters, one following so closely on the other, were doubtless puzzled and annoyed.

Harris made the same desperate excuse to Alcock: "It's all been a misunderstanding."

He knew, however, that simply saying the incident had been a misunderstanding lacked credibility. If a misunderstanding had indeed existed, Harris must supply a reason for it. In the latter part of his letter, he presented a lengthy argument for increasing Heusken's salary. Heusken, he said, envied the higher salaries of the British interpreters. This had led to the misunderstanding and his subsequent unfortunate conduct.

Among the members of the British mission, Alcock's salary was the highest: £1,600 per annum, which at a rate of four dollars to the pound, was equivalent to $6,400. The Japanese secretary received £500 ($2,000), the first assistant, £405 ($1,620), and the student-interpreters, £200 ($800). Heusken's annual salary was $1,500.

But the British government forbade all diplomatic personnel in Japan to engage in trade on their own accounts, either directly or indirectly, or to become the agent of a private firm.

At this time, little distinction was made between diplomats and merchants. The lack of such a distinction strongly affected the conduct of diplomacy and gave rise to varied abuses. In line with its policy toward Japan, the British government did not allow its diplomats to pursue commercial activities but raised their salaries by way of compensation. Many foreign service officers decided to come to Japan specifically for the higher salaries. Therefore, Heusken's salary was nearly equivalent to that of his British counterparts, and was by no means low.

Harris, nevertheless, used Heusken's salary to distract the State Department from his real reason for leaving his post:

"I respectfully inform you that I cannot retain the services of Mr. Heusken or procure a competent person in his place for less than $2,500 per annum, and I trust that you will be pleased to authorize me to pay that sum."

This letter had its intended effect: beginning from January 1, 1860—the following year—Heusken's annual salary was raised to $2,500. This flap, caused by Harris's greed, ended with Heusken receiving an unexpected bonus.

Harris had had a long history of financial scrapes, one that had begun in New York, where he was born and raised.

Harris had originally run a crockery store in New York with his elder brother, John, who was in charge of buying china and earthenware in London. Harris's heavy drinking, however, drove the business nearly into ruin. When his brother finally wrote demanding that the partnership be dissolved and added that he would return from London and run the business himself, Harris absconded with the store's money and headed for East Asia by way of San Francisco.

Once there, Harris made his way as a supercargo—a humble itinerant trader who bought goods in one port and sold them in another.

A supercargo lived from day to day, with no savings or permanent home. As he approached fifty, Harris began to think of the future: he did not want to be a lowly supercargo, roaming the seas, for the rest of his life. He started to consider a new line of profession. Should he return to New York and try his luck there? But an encounter with his brother was likely to have unfortunate consequences. The only place he could work was East Asia, where he knew the ropes and had many friends and associates.

Initially, his aim was to become a consul at one of the open ports on the China coast, but when Perry opened Japan to the world, Harris changed his plans. Returning to the United States, he campaigned energetically for the post of consul general to Japan. Fortunately for Harris, his brother had died by this time and could not interfere.

Harris did not achieve his goal easily, however. In a letter to one of Harris's friends, Secretary of State William Marcy commented that "the President is hesitating."

Harris did not have a suitable background for a diplomat: he had never studied or practiced law. President Franklin Pierce may have perceived Harris as just another unemployed job seeker without the proper qualifications. If so, his concern was well founded.

But the dearth of other qualified candidates forced Pierce to appoint Harris to the post of consul general and send him to Japan.

Other than his annual salary, which had been paid in advance, Harris did not have a cent in savings. In fact, he was deeply in debt. He went to Japan hoping to raise enough money to pay off his debts and earn a nest egg for his old age.

Japan was the perfect country for Harris. His annual salary as consul general—$5,000—was exceedingly generous compared with the $1,000 paid a consul on the China coast. At this time, European diplomats moonlighted as traders. Harris, however, could not expect to do much business in Shimoda.

Consuls also had a side income from the port entry fees levied on ships from their home countries that sailed into port. But ships rarely came to Shimoda.

The most important reason for fixing Harris's annual salary at $5,000 was concern that the Japanese might triple prices for foreigners, as they had in Perry's time.

When the Japanese, in negotiating the currency question, agreed to exchange currency weight-for-weight, Harris's cost of living fell to one-third. Penniless and in debt, Harris could now accumulate savings—his one indispensable "friend" in his old age.

He left for Japan excited with the expectation of profits to come but worried that the Japanese might not give him what he wanted. He was not disappointed. For Harris, Japan was just as Marco Polo had described it: "the land of gold, Cipangu."

But now Harris's ruthless quest for gold had finally been exposed.

In Shanghai, Harris had sold his cobangs to Augustine Heard & Company.

E. M. Dorr, the man Harris had brought with him from Shanghai to serve as vice-consul in Kanagawa, was also employed as an agent for Augustine Heard. It would be more accurate to say that Harris had purposely appointed an agent of Augustine Heard to the post of vice-consul. The advantage was mutual—for Dorr, it was much more prestigious to have the title of vice-consul than to be a mere merchant engaged in trade. Through their dealings in cobangs, the two men developed a mutually profitable relationship.

But even though Harris had made the people at Augustine Heard & Company solemnly promise never to speak of his cobang dealings, the rumors proved hard to stifle and were soon being whispered throughout the American community in Shanghai, finally reaching the ears of U.S. government investigators.

The United States government was appalled. What on earth was Harris trying to do? It was as though they had sent one thief to catch another. Charging Harris with suspicion of improper conduct, the government sent the letter relieving him of his investigation into the misdeeds of the *Powhatan*'s officers and crew.

Harris was shocked: even though he had taken every precaution, the government had somehow found him out. Rereading the order dismissing him from the investigation, Harris shuddered. His avaricious secret self had been revealed to the world.

When Harris had first come to Japan, he had never dreamed he would be the first to sign a commercial treaty with the Japanese. He presumed that that honor would go to Sir John Bowring, the British minister plenipotentiary, who was supposed to come to Japan soon after Harris stepped ashore at Shimoda. But the outbreak of the Arrow War prevented Bowring from leaving China, and the glory of concluding the first commercial treaty with Japan fell to Harris. His achievement would become an indelible part of Japanese history. If not for this unexpected besmirching, his name would have gone down in history with laurels.

How should he respond if the government asked him to explain the situation, which it was certain to do? What should he do if he received a reprimand or warning? Harris had to come up with a plausible alibi. Heusken's death, which occurred soon after, was a kind of blessing. If nothing else, it sealed his accomplice's lips.

Harris still had to determine how much his colleagues knew.

He was certain that word of his doings had reached Washington via Shanghai. What about the British minister? The French minister? Had they heard? If they had, they would be even more hostile to him than before because they would know that he had been buying cobangs from the Japanese since before the start of treaty negotiations and the Yokohama gold rush. They might be whispering that even now. In any case, they would doubtless find out sooner or later. Harris began to grow desperate.

Finally, he came up with a plausible excuse: what if he had received the cobangs as a favor, a present from the Japanese government? He had not asked for them himself. That, he hoped, might be the avenue of escape he was looking for.

He had no idea whether it would convince his government or his colleagues, but it represented his best hope. He would have to change his attitude and become more friendly toward the Japanese government. In return, they might well present him with cobangs as a token of friendship. At least, he had to make others think it was possible. It was not too late to start.

He was just about to begin his show of friendship when Heusken was killed. On the day of the funeral, Alcock proposed a meeting of the ministers from the five treaty nations. Harris understood what Alcock hoped to accomplish by this meeting. By all rights, Harris should have called it himself. But instead he followed his newly hatched plan: he made a great show of supporting the Japanese government and opposing Alcock. Harris was well aware that his position was unnatural and the arguments he advanced to defend it were farfetched. Even so, he stubbornly stuck to his guns. In the end, he reluctantly parted company with the others and remained behind in Edo. Thus, his life of maddening isolation had begun.

✳

In Yokohama, the British and other foreign merchants greeted Alcock with cold stares.

Foreigners in Yokohama, led by the British merchants, had recently organized the Yokohama Club, whose rules expressly forbade entry to officers of the British legation and consulate.

They cast a hostile eye at Alcock and barred him from their club because he had had his official letter to Vyse circulated among British merchants in Yokohama and then, to further chastise them, had it printed in the *North China Herald*.

Now that profits from buying and selling cobangs had declined, foreign merchants in Yokohama would not even look at them. Alcock, however, had harshly criticized the foreign merchants, calling them "Jews" and complaining that they were so busy hunting for cobangs that they had completely abandoned normal trade. The foreign merchants did not take this abuse lying down. To a man, they rose up in protest. Many even wrote letters to the *North China Herald*.

But the letter that made the greatest impression was contributed by an anonymous Dutchman from Nagasaki, not Yokohama.

> The merchants came to Japan to make money. When they first arrived they found that the currency was being exchanged and that this exchange was permitted under the provisions of the treaties. This included the purchase of gold, which was not prohibited in the least. They paid handsomely for this gold, at exactly the price demanded. They then sent the gold they had bought to China. What was shameful about that? It was not the part of the merchants to warn or advise the Japanese government concerning the harmfulness of this trade. Therefore, I do not

think that it is something for which foreigners in
Japan should be criticized.

The anonymous Dutchman thus defended the actions of
the foreign merchants, saying that Alcock's criticisms of them
were unfounded.

> The problem lies elsewhere. Was it right for the
> envoys of European nations not to say anything to the
> Japanese government? Shouldn't they have tried to
> stop the trade sooner? I think that they knew the
> situation. Why didn't the diplomatic representatives
> do anything? I do not want to pursue this point too
> far. Perhaps many of the diplomatic representatives,
> occupied as they were with a succession of new tasks,
> did not notice.

In his last sentence the writer seemed to be implying that
the diplomats had been protecting their own profits from cobang speculation. And that, in fact, had been the case.

The anonymous Dutchman also had something to say about
the currency question:

> The Japanese government claimed that engraving the
> ichibu with the government stamp tripled its value.
> And that was correct, after a fashion. Just as the
> government said, the ichibu was a substitute currency,
> like paper notes. Therefore, the diplomatic represen-
> tatives were wrong to demand that the ichibu and
> dollar be exchanged weight-for-weight. Exchanging
> currency by that method would inflict unfair losses
> on the Japanese.

Some of the foreign merchants in Yokohama began to say
that this anonymous Dutchman might just be right.

Harris, however, had said that no nation had ever managed
to accomplish such a thing since the history of the world began.
The Japanese, he had claimed, would not be able to prevent

counterfeiting, no matter how severely they punished offenders. The Dutchman was saying that the Japanese government was in fact doing what Harris had claimed was impossible. The Yokohama merchants began to support the Dutchman's views. That disturbed Alcock greatly.

One more thought occurred to him. Harris's arguments had once struck him as airtight. But what the Dutchman was saying also made sense, at least hypothetically. By raising the value of gold and establishing the same gold-to-silver ratio as other nations, the Japanese had finally solved the currency problem. But they had been too slow to act. So much gold had flowed out of the country that the Japanese had nearly given up hope. Alcock, however, could not bear to pursue this line of thought to its logical, painful conclusion.

✳

Alcock managed to incur the resentment of the foreign merchants in Yokohama not only for the reasons mentioned above but also for invoking a special diplomatic privilege that, by a strange alchemy, heightened feelings against him even further.

In the closing days of the Edo Period the Japanese adopted what was, in effect, a "floating exchange-rate system," just as the United States and other nations did in 1971, when they cut their currencies free of their gold "anchor" and let them float on world foreign exchange markets.

The currency float began soon after the Bakufu stopped exchanging 10,000 ichibus per day, using the pretext of the palace fire. Yokohama had been a lively hive of commercial activity until the exchange of ichibus had been halted. But no one could buy goods without ichibus. Trade was unidirectional: goods flowed from Japanese to foreign merchants and money (i.e., ichibus) flowed from the foreigners to the Japanese. Japanese merchants almost always had ichibus on hand. Foreign merchants, in turn, tried to buy them. Thus, the buying and selling of ichibus began, with the market price of ichibus changing from day to day.

On February 21, 1860, the Japanese government raised the

price of gold. Soon after this hike, $100 bought about 270 ichibus.

On a weight-for-weight basis, $100 was worth 311 ichibus. The dollar had fallen because Japanese merchants did not always want to sell ichibus, even though they still had plenty, and foreign merchants still wanted to buy them. Also, the Japanese retained their aversion to dollars, which were rarely seen outside the open ports. This was about one year before Alcock withdrew to Yokohama.

The dollar continued to sink steadily. Three months later, in May, $100 dropped to 250 ichibus. Harris, Alcock, and Bellecourt, who were all still on good terms at that time, felt the situation had come to a head.

The Japanese customs authorities (the Edo Period tax office) were obliged by the currency article of the commercial treaties to exchange currency weight-for-weight for a period of one year only, after which time the diplomatic representatives in Edo could obtain ichibus only by going to Yokohama and exchanging dollars at the money changers. The exchange rate in Yokohama was 250 ichibus to $100. The diplomats had thus suffered a loss of 60 ichibus per $100.

On May 18, 1860, with only one month to go before the one-year period stipulated in the treaties ended, Alcock met with Wakisaka and Ando and asked for permission to exchange $2,500 per month for legation use, beginning July 1—the first anniversary of the opening of the ports.

"One hundred dollars is worth three hundred and eleven ichibus," said Alcock. "Let's say that you set aside eleven ichibus, or about four percent, for reminting expenses. All you have to do is remint dollars into ichibus. You will not suffer any loss."

The Bakufu was about to ask for a delay in the opening of the two ports and two cities. The Japanese agreed to Alcock's request so that he would view their own more favorably. The Bakufu and the diplomatic representatives exchanged the following protocol:

"First, $2,500 per month will be reminted into ichibus and

transferred to the legation in Edo and the consulate in Kanagawa to supply their needs.

"Second, every three months, $3,000, or $1,000 per month,
will be reminted into ichibus and transferred to the consulates
in Nagasaki and Hakodate to supply their needs."

This protocol established a diplomatic privilege that had
the magical property of transforming dollars into ichibus.

After this, the exchange value of $100 climbed to 290
ichibus, but fell sharply to 235 ichibus at the end of July, after
which it leveled off at the 200 mark, where it stayed for some
time. This was followed by a period when it hovered between
200 and 250 ichibus. Only Alcock and the other diplomats had
the privilege of exchanging $100 for 300 ichibus under the
protocol. But what did this privilege mean?

Consider the extended period during which $100 was worth
200 ichibus.

Diplomats had the privilege of exchanging $100 for 300
ichibus. Suppose one exchanged $100 for 300 ichibus through
the Bakufu, although the market rate was $100 for 200 ichibus.
If the diplomat took his 300 ichibus to a money changer in
Yokohama, he could sell them for $150. His original capital was
$100. His profit was thus $50—fifty percent. All he had to do
was change dollars for ichibus at the special diplomatic rate and
then sell them at the market rate.

The exchange limit for the legation in Edo and the consulate in Kanagawa was $2,500 per month. If the legation staff
conducted the above-mentioned manipulations, they could turn
a profit of $1,250 every month. At the British and French
legations, this money was distributed to the staff in proportion
to their salaries. Ernest Satow, a young British diplomat who
came to Japan while Alcock was on leave in England and eventually became fluent in Japanese, wrote about this period in his
memoirs, *A Diplomat in Japan*:

> Where the money came from that was thus transferred
> to the pockets of officials can be best explained by those
> who are versed in economical questions. For my own part,

I cannot look back on that period without shame, and my only excuse, which is perhaps of little worth in the court of history, is that I was at the bottom of the ladder, and received the proportion paid to me by those who were in charge of the business.

In the case of America, however, in place of "legation" and "consulate," the protocol read: "Two thousand five hundred dollars per month shall be reminted and transferred to the minister in Edo and the consul in Kanagawa to supply their needs."

Who decided this? Harris, of course. When he drafted the American protocol, Heusken was still alive. According to this protocol, Heusken did not have the right to exchange even one yen at the special rate. This oversight may have been a point of contention between Heusken and Harris. After Heusken's death, Harris was able to use this privilege as he pleased.

Harris, a minister, received $1,500 of the allotted $2,500 and Dorr, a consul, $1,000. When the exchange rate was 200 ichibus to $100, Harris could thus earn $750 a month or $9,000 a year. Dorr's earnings were $500 a month or $6,000 a year. Of course, the exchange rate did not remain at 2 to 1 indefinitely. But even when the rate rose to 230 ichibus to $100, Harris could make $5,400 a year and Dorr, $3,600.

Harris's annual salary was $5,000. Financially, he was a very fortunate man.

The British legation in Edo and the consulate in Kanagawa had a total staff of six. The allotted $2,500 was paid out in proportion to their salaries. Alcock's salary was $6,400 (£1,600). It was raised to this level both to put him on a par with Harris and to compensate him for being forbidden to engage in trade. The Japanese secretary, who was second in rank, received $2,000, the first assistant, $1,600, and the student interpreters, $800 annually. Alcock's share, which was calculated in proportion to his salary, enabled him to clear a profit of about forty percent. When the exchange rate was 200 ichibus to $100 he could make $3,600 a year, and when it was 230 ichibus, $2,100.

Although this did not equal Harris's profit, it was a substantial sum.

It had not been his intention, but Alcock had in effect created an absurdly unfair diplomatic privilege. Private citizens, particularly the foreign merchants in Yokohama, were not about to overlook this "unfair advantage." Having been so severely handled by Alcock for their buying of cobangs, they nursed a grudge against him that bordered on hatred. They criticized Alcock harshly in the *North China Herald.*

The anonymous Dutchman from Nagasaki fired the following salvo in support of their anti-Alcock campaign: "If the diplomatic representatives are invoking this privilege on the pretext that the cost of living is high, they are being ridiculous. If their pay is insufficient, they should apply to their home governments for an increase."

Though he was showered with abuse, Alcock did not decline to avail himself of his new diplomatic privilege.

Yokohama was not a pleasant place for Alcock. After several unsuccessful attempts to have himself invited back to Edo by the Bakufu, he returned on his own after a month so that he could save face, if nothing else. He had gained no concrete results by withdrawing to Yokohama.

Unceremoniously reinstated in Edo, his withdrawal to Yokohama having neither resolved nor proven a thing, Alcock brooded angrily. How, he asked himself, had things reached such a pass? Despised by the foreign merchant community in Yokohama, indeed, banned from their so-called Yokohama Club! He smiled bitterly at the presumption of that pack of thieves.

The Dutchman and his cursed letter, Heusken's murder, Harris's inexplicable defection to the Japanese on every point—things were turning uglier and uglier. Alcock's ulcer had become an almost constant torment to him. God, how sick he was of the plain rice-gruel his Japanese cook incessantly put before him!

No, he told himself, I by no means regret having brought about the special higher diplomatic exchange-rate privilege. Not after what I have endured in this country. The merchants have made astronomical fortunes, and yet they dare to revile me for this. That and showing them to the world for what they are, a lot of hypocrites, he thought, his thin lips twisting into a grimace.

Alcock was finding the need to redeem himself in the eyes of the world becoming uppermost in his mind. How it galled him that a man can fulfill his duty in every particular and yet be denied the esteem he deserved while scoundrels like the merchants and Harris went unscathed. He could not trust his posthumous reputation to the ignorance of others. It was clearer than ever before—he would, indeed he must, write the definitive version of his life and work in Japan. He applied himself with renewed vigor to his daily journal entries.

6

Crossfire

W hen Alcock was appointed consul general to Japan, he made up his mind to do two things. One was to make a thorough study of the Japanese language. Once in Japan, he eagerly studied Japanese whenever he could spare time from his official duties.

The other was to write a book about Japan.

Alcock, however, was not the only foreigner to come to Japan with that ambition. Heusken, despite his lack of formal education, was another. In fact, nearly all of the reasonably literate foreigners who came to Japan at this time were potential authors. Since Perry's visit to Japan, several books about the country had appeared: the ghostwritten *Personal Journal of Commodore Matthew C. Perry*, the *Narrative of the Earl of Elgin's Mission to China and Japan* by Lawrence Oliphant, secretary to Lord Elgin, the minister plenipotentiary who negotiated Britain's commercial treaty with Japan, and *Fregat Pallada (Journal of a Voyage to Japan)* by Russian author Ivan Alexandrovitch Goncharov.

Alcock had been an early reader of Perry's *Journal* and Elgin's *Narrative*. He had also read the accounts of travel in Japan by Engelbert Kaempfer and Carl Peter Thunberg, physicians attached to the Dutch factory at Dejima.

Alcock realized, however, that these books contained nothing more than surface observations made under restricted conditions. For example, none provided satisfactory accounts of

Japan's political arrangements, feudal system, industrial development, cultural level, or such particulars as the structure of family relationships and the status of women. For a period of about seventy or eighty years before Japan closed itself off from the rest of the world at the start of the Edo Period, the Portuguese and Spanish had traveled freely about the country, recording their observations. Alcock discovered that no books of that type had been written about Japan since then.

As the diplomatic representative of Great Britain, Alcock had been favored with the opportunity to reside in Edo, the Japanese capital. He could also travel freely in the interior any time he pleased, a privilege granted only to diplomatic representatives. He was the first to enjoy such a chance since the early Portuguese and Spanish, and was eager to use it to write a book about Japan.

Although not in the habit of keeping a journal, Alcock began one so that he could jot down thoughts and impressions that might otherwise slip away.

Now that one year had passed, his journal had grown to a considerable size. Alcock was eager to be the first since the Portuguese and Spanish to publish a description of Japan as seen from the inside. He decided upon *The Capital of the Tycoon* as his working title.

Of course, he could make arrangements with a London publisher by mail, send the manuscript, and have it published sight unseen. But that would require a great deal of time and trouble. If at all possible, the best way would be to return to England and guide the book through publication himself. He could even correct the galley proofs. How else could he be sure they would get it right? Alcock began to long for a chance to return to England.

He had another reason for wanting to go home. Ever since the death of his wife in 1853, Alcock had been living alone. He was thoroughly tired of that type of life. Unfortunately, the European population in East Asia was almost entirely male. Females were either married women or their young, innocent daughters. It was nearly impossible to find a suitable partner. It would be much easier, however, in England.

As he was approaching the end of his first year in Japan, Alcock applied to his home government for a leave of absence. About this same time, he received a request from the Bakufu for a delay in the opening of the two ports and two cities.

Alcock's position regarding the treaty had remained unchanged: at all costs, first and foremost, the treaty must be fulfilled. When the Japanese government came to him with this request, however, his attitude was different. During his second meeting with Minister of Foreign Affairs Ando, Alcock announced that "the way has been cleared for you to dispatch a minister plenipotentiary to Britain to resolve the question." In other words, he was inviting the Japanese to send a minister plenipotentiary to England. Alcock hoped to use this as an opportunity to accompany the envoy and return home.

But the Bakufu vacillated and the days passed. Heusken's death, the falling out with Harris, the removal to Yokohama, and subsequent return to Edo kept Alcock totally occupied, with little time to pursue anything else.

❋

Immediately upon his return to Edo, Alcock had to retrace his steps to Yokohama and leave for Hong Kong on official business. A defendant had appealed a decision that Alcock had handed down while serving in his judicial capacity as Canton consul to a superior court in Hong Kong.

Although the superior court ruled that Alcock's decision had been legally correct, it ordered him to pay a fine of $2,000 for some trivial procedural errors. He returned to Nagasaki feeling that he had endured an incredible, thoroughly unpleasant ordeal. His first stop in Japan was Nagasaki.

It was rumored in Nagasaki's European community that the anonymous Dutchman who had written the caustic letters castigating the foreign diplomatic corps was a certain Pompe van Meerdervoort, a Dejima physician. Originally a member of the second educational corps dispatched by the Dutch government to Japan to share western learning and technology, van Meerder-voort taught western medicine to Japanese students at the Nagasaki Naval Institute. The first institution of its kind in Japan, the institute had been founded in Nagasaki in 1855. When the second educational corps returned to Holland, van Meerder-voort stayed behind and continued to teach: he played a major role in the early history of modern medicine in Japan. Among the Japanese he was known simply as "Pompe."

After landing in Nagasaki on his way back from Hong Kong, Alcock heard the rumors about the identity of the author of the letters criticizing him and the other diplomats.

Van Meerdervoort's accomplishments in Nagasaki were well known to Alcock. In addition to teaching medicine to the Japanese, he had founded a hospital where British seamen were often treated.

Alcock had once been a doctor himself. He was deeply curious about this physician who, though unknown in Europe, had come to the farthest shores of the Far East to teach modern medicine to half-civilized students, unaided and alone. Ordinarily, his would be a story that Alcock would have felt compelled to include in *The Capital of the Tycoon*. But this physician had taken sides with the Japanese government and foreign merchants against the diplomatic representatives. Alcock found him provoking beyond words. He did not make even a passing reference to van Meerdervoort's accomplishments in *The Capital of the Tycoon*. Thus Alcock had his small revenge.

Partly to be able to add color to the descriptions in *The Capital of the Tycoon*, Alcock took a leisurely trip overland from Nagasaki to Edo. He arrived back in Edo on July 1, 1861, exactly two years after the opening of the ports.

One of those who met him on his arrival was Lawrence Oliphant, the author of the *Narrative of the Earl of Elgin's Mission to China and Japan*. Oliphant, who had come to Japan three years earlier as the secretary of James Bruce—the eighth Earl of Elgin—was still a young man, though his hairline was rapidly receding. He was a cheerful, outgoing type, bursting with youthful curiosity. Three years earlier Oliphant's opposite number had been Iwase, who had negotiated the commercial treaty with Harris. At that time, just prior to his dismissal by Ii, Iwase had displayed an insatiable thirst for knowledge and enlightenment. Expressing a strong desire to study the English language, he had made a highly favorable impression on Oliphant. Also, the cost of living for foreigners had been extraordinarily low. All this had made Oliphant paint almost too rosy a picture of Japan. He had written about it as though it were a paradise.

Every time he looked into the pages of Oliphant's *Narrative*, Alcock was overcome with disgust.

He doesn't understand a thing, he thought. Oliphant had been dispatched to Japan to serve as British representative while Alcock was away on a leave of absence.

The next day Alcock quickly began preparing for his trip home. That night, however, the British legation was attacked by a large band of assassins.

Alcock escaped unharmed and the legation staff suffered no fatalities. Oliphant and the Nagasaki consul were severely wounded, however, with Oliphant receiving bad cuts on the arm and neck.

Perhaps now he understands the situation here a little better, thought Alcock, with a hint of triumph.

Ordinarily, such an attack on the British legation would have scuttled negotiations to delay the opening of the two ports and two cities. If Alcock had not been in a hurry to return to England, he would have done just that. But Alcock was determined to return home, not only to find a wife, but to ensure that his book about Japan would be the first. He could not allow himself to become entangled in the aftermath of the attack and in the negotiations to delay the opening of the two ports and two cities: he had other, higher priorities. He urged the Japanese to send a minister plenipotentiary to Europe so that he could use the Japanese mission as an excuse to return home.

Responding to Alcock's encouragement, the Bakufu decided to dispatch a diplomatic mission to Europe, and the British government agreed to receive it, partly out of curiosity: government leaders had a strong desire to meet these exotic, "half-civilized" islanders.

The Japanese mission boarded the frigate *Odin,* a steamer supplied by the British, and set off for Europe on January 23, 1862.

Alcock had planned to leave with the Japanese mission, but the orders approving his leave of absence were delayed, finally arriving in March. On receiving them, Alcock quickly completed his travel preparations and left for Yokohama.

Unfortunately, no British ships-of-war were in port. He could ask for passage aboard a trading ship, but there was the humiliating possibility that he might be refused, considering his standing among the merchants. Luckily, a Dutch man-of-war happened to be in Yokohama. The Dutch minister, de Wit, was on good terms with the captain and persuaded him to accept Alcock as a passenger. Alcock left Yokohama on March 23.

Two Japanese accompanied him, Fuchibe Tokuzo and Moriyama Takichiro. Both were high-ranking officials in the office of foreign affairs.

Moriyama had been permitted to join the trip at Alcock's strong recommendation. He was a seasoned interpreter whose career had begun with Perry's first visit to Japan. No one knew more about the Bakufu's dealings with foreigners. He had also participated in the negotiations with Harris.

Harris had often boasted to Alcock that he had signed a commercial treaty with Japan without having even a single warship. But Alcock harbored doubts as to what had in fact happened. He had requested that Moriyama be allowed to accompany him, hoping to find answers to this and many other questions.

One in particular weighed heavily on his mind: the question of whether the negotiations to delay the opening of the two ports and two cities would go smoothly. Realizing that there was no harm done in granting Alcock's request—and that it might aid the negotiations—the Japanese permitted Moriyama to go on the trip.

✳

From Shanghai, mail steamers sailed to Europe twice a month. Alcock was not on bad terms with the foreign merchants in Nagasaki. If he boarded a Shanghai-bound merchantman there, he could easily catch the mail steamer that left for Europe on April 7. Alcock thus reckoned that he would have ample time to spare. But his ship encountered strong headwinds, and even with the aid of the auxiliary steam boiler, took eleven days to reach Nagasaki, instead of the anticipated four.

When he arrived in Nagasaki, Alcock was chafing at the bit. Fortunately, he found a British gunboat stopping there on her way to Edo. The captain was laid up in Nagasaki with smallpox. With the captain away from the ship, recuperating in British Navy lodgings, Alcock was easily able to make the gunboat execute an about-face. The gunboat, with Alcock aboard, sped for Shanghai. Unfortunately, it arrived just after the regular mail steamer had departed for Europe—Alcock had missed his connection by a hair.

When a downcast Alcock disembarked, he learned that the British admiral was staying in the city, and quickly informed him of his predicament. The admiral dashed off an official letter and ordered a man-of-war to carry it and Alcock to Hong Kong in time to catch the steamer. Boarding the warship, Alcock finally overtook the Europe-bound steamer in Hong Kong.

The journal that he had been keeping daily as raw material for his book was now enormous. During the tedious two-month voyage, Alcock put it in order. He also made preparations for adding new material on a theme he had not even considered when he had first thought about writing a book: a defense— addressed to foreign merchants in Yokohama and newspaper editors in China—of his policies and actions.

Persuaded by the letters of the anonymous Dutchman, the editors of the *North China Herald* had taken a firm stand against Alcock. Recently, their anti-Alcock campaign had reached its vituperative peak. After Alcock left for England, the *Hong Kong Press* joined in the campaign. These newspapers mercilessly pilloried the now-absent Alcock in their columns. "The British envoy has unfairly obtained large profits using his ichibu exchange privilege," claimed one editorial.

Alcock's profits were minor compared with Harris's, besides which, his expenses were substantial, and he had had to pay the $2,000 fine levied on him by the superior court in Hong Kong. His fortune had actually shrunk since his arrival in Japan. Even so, Alcock was being criticized for unfair profiteering.

"He has tried to placate and curry favor with the Japanese through an endless series of spineless concessions," stormed another editorial. "The attack on the British legation was caused by personal hostility toward the British minister."

The newspaper attacks against him had escalated to a hysterical height. Alcock was being subjected to a crossfire of criticism.

Alcock did not deign to respond to his critics. Were he to deliver his rebuttal, they would once again descend on him like a pack of wolves—that much was certain. Alcock was saving his counterattack for his book. This had become one of his main motivations for completing it.

The mail steamer went as far as Pointe de Galle, Ceylon, where passengers bound for Europe had to transfer to another mail steamer. After stopping for the mail in Bombay, they crossed the Arabian Sea.

From Pointe de Galle, the heat intensified unbearably. After stopping at Aden, the ship made its way up the Red Sea. It was a voyage through a scorching hell. Even reading was nearly impossible. All he could do was talk with Moriyama, the veteran interpreter who had been serving the Bakufu since the time of Perry. Alcock realized that if he wanted Moriyama to talk, a certain finesse would be necessary. Starting in with direct questions would have caused the interpreter to withdraw even further. But since leaving Pointe de Galle, Alcock had managed to completely break down the interpreter's reserve. He intended to probe Moriyama thoroughly while he had the chance, even though the heat made every kind of effort exhausting.

By this time, Moriyama could speak Dutch like a native and English well enough to exchange ideas: no barrier existed to a mutual understanding between the two men. Alcock leisurely conducted his interviews when the sun had set and the deck had cooled or when they took their meals in the first-class dining room. Moriyama was surprisingly frank:

"For a long time we have regarded England as we would a terrible wild beast. When we signed the commercial treaty, the American minister told us that our concern was not misplaced and that England was actually even more frightening than we had feared. Therefore, we quickly concluded the treaty with the American minister to give us a shield against England."

Harris had frequently boasted of having concluded a commercial treaty with Japan without receiving any kind of material aid or using any kind of coercive measures. In short, he had achieved a victory of reason, argument, and diplomatic skill. Listening to Moriyama, Alcock began to piece together what had actually motivated the Japanese to sign. At the time, of course, England had been thrashing China in the Arrow War.

That night Alcock wrote in his journal:

> By stressing the threat of the allied expeditionary force, Harris was able to win advantage and prestige for the United States. It was just as though he had invaded the country without spending a single penny. On the other hand, all that England gained was an unsavory reputation as a demanding, bellicose nation. Harris is truly a genius.

Moriyama, however, did not tell Alcock everything. He did not tell Alcock that Harris had badgered him in bringing three, then five, then ten cobangs to the American consulate. He also neglected to tell Alcock about the Kichi episode. While Harris was in Shimoda, he had asked Moriyama to procure a woman. Moriyama communicated Harris's request to the local authorities, who then ordered low-ranking officials to pay a certain Kichi to go, unwillingly, to Harris. After only three days he tired of the woman and dismissed her. That was fine with Moriyama, but Harris begrudged them the money he had promised and stalled for four months before paying it.

After beginning his solitary existence in Edo, Harris had taken a divorced woman from Zenpukuji Temple to his room on the condition that she stay just one night. Moriyama knew all the particulars of this incident as well, but did not mention them to Alcock.

Also, when Harris was still at Shimoda, he had shown Moriyama Perry's *Journal*. Before Perry's arrival, Moriyama had spoken casually in broken English with a sailor aboard the *Preble*, which had come to Nagasaki to pick up shipwrecked whalers.

Hearing that there was an interesting Dutch interpreter aboard who could speak English and liked champagne, the author of the *Journal* had gone to meet him. Taking an instant liking to Moriyama, he had mentioned him in a journal entry. When he saw this description of himself, Moriyama was surprised, but was even more astonished when, on returning to Edo, he learned that Perry's *Journal* had already been rendered into Japanese by the Edo office of translation.

When Harris arrived in Japan, however, the *Journal* had not yet been published. It came into his hands via Washington, Hong Kong, Hakodate, Edo, and Shimoda. Before turning the *Journal* over to Harris, the Bakufu—or, more precisely, Hotta—had kept it in Edo for four months and had it translated. Of course, the translators at the office of translation and Hotta, who saw their work, knew of Moriyama's words and actions. The Bakufu did not permit its interpreters to engage in private conversations with foreigners. They were wary of these men who had mastered a foreign tongue and were therefore capable of carrying on secret business with the "enemy."

Had this incident occurred during Ii's rule, Moriyama would have been severely punished. Fortunately for him, Hotta was in charge. Moriyama's services were essential for conducting the negotiations with Harris. Also, Hotta was not particularly troubled about Moriyama's slip of the tongue and never criticized him for it.

During Ii's regime, Moriyama had kept himself in check

and behaved with greater caution. Now Ii was gone and Kuze and Ando were in charge. The new Bakufu leaders had created a brighter, freer atmosphere, but Moriyama knew a sudden reversal coulld occur at any time. He remained on his guard, even during the trip to Europe.

It had been a long voyage. At times, he was tempted to unburden himself to Alcock. But if he spoke carelessly, the British minister might write a book that would be translated and read by top-ranking government officials. If that happened, Moriyama would really be in trouble. Therefore, he meted out his information carefully.

Although he was uncertain as to what Moriyama was really thinking, Alcock was favorably impressed by the interpreter's reserved, silent bearing: it was very samurailike. As an Englishman, he found it far preferable to flattery or fawning overfamiliarity. Alcock did not press Moriyama to make involuntary revelations.

Disembarking at Suez, Alcock journeyed overland to Alexandria via Cairo. At Alexandria he boarded a ship that stopped at Malta, a British colony. Disembarking at Marseilles, he traveled by train through France, crossed the English Channel and arrived in London on May 30.

Among European nations, compensation for concessions was a basic rule of diplomacy.

British officials told the Japanese mission that if England were to grant them a delay in the opening of the two ports and two cities, it would expect something in return. The Japanese responded by offering to reduce tariff rates and remove various barriers to trade.

While these negotiations were in progress, the Japanese stubbornly attempted to carry out rather strange instructions from their home government. The instructions ordered them to "gain the approval of the treaty nations for the withdrawal of the ichibu and the circulation of a half ichibu one-and-a-half times heavier."

Their instructions, which had already been prepared when Alcock landed at Yokohama, were to seek approval for the circulation of a coin identical to the nishu, the coin which had been withdrawn soon after it was issued amid a storm of foreign criticism. The Bakufu had surely had a purpose in giving the diplomatic mission these instructions. Alcock, however, did not understand what that purpose was and did not try very hard to do so. Later, he casually presented the instructions, with relevant documents attached, to the Treasury and asked for their opinion.

In return for offering various types of compensation, the Japanese mission obtained approval for a five-year delay in opening the two ports and two cities and concluded what came to be known as the London Protocol. The mission, together with Moriyama, then left for Holland, the next country on their itinerary, on June 12.

✳

Meanwhile Harris, having become more intimate with the Bakufu—and estranged from his fellow westerners—after his 180-degree shift in attitude, was living a life of utter isolation in Edo. Now that his home government was about to find out about his cobang profiteering in Shimoda, his only thought was how to escape from Japan.

But where could he go? He had many friends in Hong Kong, Canton, and Macao. But those places were all too close to Edo, Yokohama, and Shanghai. Word of his misdeeds might easily follow him there.

The isolation was unendurable. He had to find a place of refuge where he had friends and where his cobang profiteering would not come back to haunt him. That place could only be New York, where he had been born and raised. Luckily, the only obstacle to his plans—his elder brother—had been removed long ago.

While in Shimoda, Harris had saved enough money to live on for the rest of his life. Although he continued to turn a tidy profit by exercising his diplomatic ichibu exchange privilege, when he tired of his solitary existence in Edo, Harris lost no time in asking his home government to recall him.

He did not want to resign, but to be recalled. For Harris, ever on the lookout for his own economic advantage, the difference was crucial. If he were to submit his resignation, he would not only cease to draw his salary as soon as it was accepted but have to pay seven or eight hundred dollars out of his own pocket for travel expenses. Were he to be recalled, however, the American government would take care of everything.

In April 1861, when Harris thought his request should be reaching the authorities, the United States was thrown into turmoil by civil war. Abraham Lincoln succeeded James Buchanan as president and William H. Seward replaced Lewis Cass as secretary of state. The U.S. government, which had been about to reprimand Harris, now had no time to bother with a minister to a small unknown country on the other side of the world. It neither reprimanded him, recalled him, nor answered his request.

Undeterred, Harris dispatched a second request, which also went unanswered. He was finally forced to submit his resignation. On July 10, nine days after the attack on the British legation, Harris sent his letter of resignation to President Lincoln. He could not wait any longer: even if he had to pay his own way, he wanted to leave Japan as soon as possible and return home.

Harris gave poor health and advanced age as his reasons for resigning. These were thin excuses.

Born in 1804, Harris had been nearly fifty-two when he took up his post in Shimoda—not a young man even then. When he wrote his letter of resignation, he was fifty-six years and nine months old—not that much older than when he had first arrived.

His health had been indifferent even before he had come to Japan. Before concluding the treaty, he had suffered a near-fatal illness. Thus neither of the reasons he advanced for his resignation represented new developments.

The day after penning his letter of resignation, Harris wrote the following about the attack on the British legation in a dispatch that he sent by separate envelope:

There is a party in this country who is opposed
to the presence of any foreigners in Japan, and, in
addition to this there is a very strong dislike to the
English in particular, which feeling seems to attach
especially to Mr. Alcock. He was absent from this city
for some three months, during which time the utmost
quiet prevailed; yet within thirty-six hours of his
return the attack in question was made on him.

I am happy to say that these prejudices do not
extend to our citizens in this country, and I think I
am personally popular among all classes of Japanese.

In actuality, the Japanese attacks were not directed at the
Americans, the British, or a particular British minister, but were
indiscriminate. The British minister had made himself conspic-
uous by traveling about the country gathering "color" for his
book, and from the viewpoint of the attackers, the staff of the
British legation contained the most "game." It was for that
reason that they were chosen as the targets of the attack. Both
of Harris's claims were unfounded: that the Japanese distin-
guished between British and Americans, and that he himself was
"personally popular." Here he was also implying that it would
have been entirely natural for such a popular fellow to receive a
present of cobangs from the Japanese.

This dispatch was not of pressing interest to U.S. government officials. For those who knew the real situation, however, it
was a joke. Harris had started speculating in cobangs soon after
coming to Shimoda. That had been disgraceful enough, but
even worse was the fact that U.S. citizens in Yokohama had
petitioned for Harris's dismissal.

They rightly claimed that "the minister has done nothing
either directly or indirectly to serve American citizens living in
Yokohama or help them uphold their treaty rights."

They also demanded the dismissal of Dorr for the same
reason.

Soon after arriving in Yokohama, Harris had entrusted
Dorr with all matters related to the city. A proud and haughty

man, Harris regarded the citizens of Yokohama as beneath him. Dorr, however, had little time to spare for his duties as vice-consul: although he was later to sever his connection with the company, at this point he was exclusively occupied with his work as the agent of the trading firm of Augustine Heard & Company.

The two men did work diligently to enrich themselves through cobang profiteering, however. But their efforts in this line did little to make them "personally popular" among their fellow Americans in Yokohama.

Harris confined himself in Edo, not daring to leave. A sociable man, Harris found the isolation hard to bear. He often complained of his difficult situation in letters to the widow of a friend from his Hong Kong days, Kate Drinker, and her daughter. The day that he drafted his letter of resignation to President Lincoln, he also wrote to Mrs. Drinker:

> You have no doubt heard the news of the murder of my secretary, Mr. Heusken, last January. [Here Harris brazenly defended his decision to oppose the other diplomatic representatives.] This affair has broken off all intercourse between me & the French and English legations, which makes my position here a very isolated one—I go down to Kanagawa once in a while and visit the Missionary ladies (there are three families) who are very agreeable persons, but with this exception, my life is almost as isolated as it was while living at Shimoda.

In Shimoda Harris had had Heusken for companionship. Other than Heusken, who spoke only broken English, his only "friend" had been Moriyama. There had also been Inoue Kiyono, the Prince of Shinano and governor of Shimoda, who would usually listen to him if he ranted and raved long enough. In Edo, however, he had no one to talk to. Day after day, Harris tasted the hellish bitterness of isolation.

During this time, Harris's demeanor toward the Japanese

government had changed completely. Indeed, he had no alternative but to ally himself with the Bakufu. When Bakufu officials consulted him, he had to respond with at least a show of sincerity and warmth.

Harris had quickly agreed to a delay in the opening of the ports and asked the U.S. government to grant its approval. When the government consented, the Bakufu came to trust and respect Harris even more. In a letter to Harris, Minister of Foreign Affairs Ando modestly asserted that "we trust you as we would a teacher." As history has recorded, Harris became known as the Bakufu's advisor and "benefactor."

Enduring the pain of isolation, Harris continued to lie low in Edo until he could make his escape from Japan. He had long ago sullied the lofty reputation he had earned for his diplomatic labors. He had paid a high price for the cobangs he had collected on the sly in Shimoda, never dreaming he might be found out.

※

Harris's resignation was accepted. His replacement, Robert Hewson Pruyn, together with the new Kanagawa consul, George S. Fisher, arrived in Japan on April 25, 1862. Pruyn was a fitting successor to Harris: he was later to embezzle money that the Bakufu advanced him for the purchase of a warship. The U.S. government apparently had a predilection for sending unsavory characters to the newly opened Japan. Harris turned over his duties to Pruyn and left Japan on May 8, one month and a half after Alcock's departure for England.

Following in Alcock's footsteps, Harris headed home via Europe. Although he worried that Moriyama might say something "unexpected" to Alcock, Harris reassured himself that it wouldn't matter even if he did: he was putting Japan behind him, never to return.

Many travelers sailing to America from Europe, including Harris, boarded steamers leaving from Liverpool. On the way, Harris stopped off in London, but did not call on Alcock, who was there at the time.

Instead, he quietly departed for his old hometown, New York. Upon arriving, he left immediately for Washington to finalize his resignation.

At this time, Americans bragged of Harris's Treaty of Edo and Perry's Treaty of Kanagawa as the greatest diplomatic coups in America's brief history.

Two years earlier, the young nation had enthusiastically welcomed the Japanese mission when it came to Washington to exchange instruments of ratification. The newspapers were full of news about the exotic visitors. Harris had produced and promoted this event, which had so deeply stirred and excited the American people. Moreover, Harris's treaty, which had been concluded by one man alone, without the aid of a single warship, would shine on in the annals of American diplomacy.

This kind of success story flattered Americans' view of themselves. Some scholars have written that, after his return, Harris and his achievement faded into oblivion because America was in the midst of a civil war. Actually, the opposite is true. At the height of the war, when Americans were pitted brother against brother in a mortal struggle for the future of the nation, Harris—the great treaty maker between the United States and Japan—should by all rights have been the center of attention. President Lincoln would ordinarily have led the nation in extolling the hero who had accomplished such tremendous deeds. But this did not happen.

Harris, the great hero, had secretly committed an act— cobang profiteering—that hard-working, God-fearing Americans considered despicable.

In the confusion of wartime, the ever-lucky Harris managed to escape chastisement, but officials in the State Department were aware of his misdeeds. Also, they had by this time received the petition from the U.S. citizens in Yokohama calling for their minister's dismissal. They thus gave Harris a chilly reception. After hastily announcing his resignation to official Washington, Harris returned to New York and took up residence on

Fourth Avenue.

Now in utter disgrace with his government, Harris firmly clung to the one "friend"—his savings—that would never fail him. Harris settled in to a comfortable retirement, his fortune made.

After seeing the Japanese mission safely off to Holland, Alcock began to write his long-planned book, The Capital of the Tycoon. *While so occupied, he was also able to accomplish the second goal of his trip back to England: he met and became engaged to the widow of a missionary.*

All in all, the writing of the book was an extremely satisfying interlude for Alcock. After his many years in the Far East, it was soothing to sleep in an English bed, eat well-cooked English food and drink lovely claret. And he found the act of writing itself to be an excellent balm for his overwrought nerves: as the author, he and he alone controlled the creation of a world.

By the end of 1862 The Capital of the Tycoon *had been completed, proofed, and printed. All that remained was to bind it. Alcock eagerly anticipated its publication, when he would be covered in glory as the first European to write in-depth on Japan in the last two hundred fifty years. He felt fitter than he had in ages.*

7

Revenge

One day in late December, Alcock received a summons from an official of the Exchequer. He wished to discuss the currency question, about which Alcock had inquired nearly half a year earlier.

The Japanese diplomatic mission had stubbornly insisted on fulfilling Mizuno's instructions to "gain the approval of the treaty nations for the withdrawal of the ichibu and the circulation of a half ichibu one-and-a-half times heavier." Not understanding the meaning of these instructions, Alcock had casually sent a letter of inquiry, along with the relevant documents, to the Treasury, after which he put the matter out of his mind.

The one who had summoned him was George Arbuthnot, a Treasury official and an influential expert on banking and currency. On December 24 Arbuthnot finally finished writing his *Report on the Japanese Currency to Lords of the Treasury*.

What could he have to tell me? wondered Alcock as he left for the Treasury.

Arbuthnot greeted Alcock cordially. "First, I'd like to apologize for the delay in completing my report. This is a rather difficult problem. Let me first tell you my conclusion," he continued. "The Japanese claims concerning the currency question seem to be essentially correct."

The Japanese had claimed that the ichibu's actual value was not defined by its silver content and was effectively tripled by engraving the coin with a government stamp. In effect, Arbuthnot was saying that the Dutch doctor in Nagasaki and the Europeans in Yokohama were right. Alcock had heard this opinion before.

"I see," said Alcock. "In other words, you are saying the Japanese government has done what no other country in the world has been able to do."

"So it would seem," said Arbuthnot. He did not mince words but continued, saying, "The confusion in the Japanese currency system has been the direct result of coercive actions by the foreign representatives, who have consistently ignored the views of the Japanese side."

Alcock blanched: he was one of those foreign representatives—in fact, he was their leader.

"You have probably heard about the flow of cobangs out of the country," said Alcock. "After arriving in Edo, I and the other foreign representatives immediately advised the Japanese government to triple the value of the cobang. If the Japanese government had followed that advice, the outflow of cobangs would not have occurred and the confusion could have been avoided."

Alcock defended himself with a rising desperation. Arbuthnot waited for him to finish and then quietly continued:

"That was a mistake. I would like to explain why, point by point. Please don't misunderstand: I did not call you here today with the intent of criticizing you. You and the American minister fully deserve censure for your actions, but I would like to set all that aside for the moment. I would like you to listen so that you may know the truth of the matter."

Alcock fixed Arbuthnot with a frozen stare, hoping to intimidate him into silence. But Arbuthnot proceeded undeterred.

"My report concludes that the provision for the weight-for-weight exchange of currency in Article Ten of the British treaty violates various basic international principles and flouts accepted standards of behavior among European nations. My grounds for making such a statement are described in detail in the report. I urge you to read it. To be frank, many of the facts that I have

learned reflect on the honor of you and other diplomatic representatives, but I have kept those facts confidential.

"As you know, official documents of this nature are filed
and depending on the circumstances, made public in one or two
years. We do this because we cannot predict what would happen
if the Japanese were to see this report and learn the truth. They
would probably not stop with a demand for redress. If this
matter is not carefully handled, it could lead to a rupture of
diplomatic relations. In other words, Mr. Alcock, it could harm
the national interest. If the Japanese government were to try
other means—such as appealing to international opinion—not
only would the national interest be affected, but you and the
other diplomatic representatives in Japan, as well as high-ranking foreign office officials, would become, at best, a laughingstock.

"You must understand this, sir. You have not only served as
Her Majesty's first representative in Japan—you have been reap-
pointed to the same post. It would be too absurd if you were to
remain ignorant of the truth. It would also be unfair to the
Japanese government."

Alcock had not yet grasped the full import of what Arbuthnot was telling him, but he did understand that the problems he
had caused had been brought before the bar, as it were, and that
a harsh judgment had been handed down against him.

"When Commodore Perry visited Japan, the Japanese
claimed that they had tripled the value of the ichibu by engraving it with the government stamp. Later, they retracted that
claim, then reasserted it. In short, they bungled repeatedly. Let
us set aside for a moment the question of why they made those
blunders. When you and the other diplomatic representatives
arrived in Yokohama, they made the same claim and prepared a
coin called the nishu.

"You and the American minister asserted that no country in
the history of the world had ever managed to successfully increase the value of its currency with a mere stamp. You claimed
that if the Japanese were to try it, counterfeiting would immediately become rampant and that, in the end, they would fail. But

what would happen if silver were not in the hands of ordinary citizens, which happens to be the case in Japan?

"Until trade under the commercial treaties began, Holland's monopoly trade with Japan was supervised by the Japanese government and, prior to that, by the Dutch East India Company. According to the company's records, the Japanese government has been importing gold and silver, particularly silver, via Holland and China for nearly one hundred years. These precious metals are used exclusively for coinage. Surely you've noticed that the Japanese do not adorn themselves with jewelry, nor do they eat with metal implements, as we do. When the Spanish and Portuguese were free to travel about Japan, it was a gold- and silver-producing country, but later the amount of gold and silver mined declined rapidly. Therefore, Japan continues to import these metals.

"But despite this decline, what do you think would happen if the government were still to have exclusive possession of the mining and sales rights for gold and silver? Common citizens would not be able to make counterfeit coins, even if they wanted to—that's what would happen, sir.

"Allow me to state my conclusion first: the Japanese were correct. The value of the ichibu was indeed tripled by engraving it with the government stamp. The minister of foreign affairs told you and the others that the ichibu was an auxiliary currency, like paper and leather notes. He also said that it would be impossible to exchange ichibus and dollars weight-for-weight. You understand now, don't you?"

Alcock did not reply.

"For example, say we have a paper or leather note—either will do—with 'ten pounds' written on it. Let us also say that this paper or leather note is official tender. But even if it weighs as much as one Mexican dollar, that one dollar is not the same as ten pounds. The same logic applies in this case. There may have been some confusion because the ichibu and dollar are both silver, but why did you not at least listen to the Japanese government's explanation, which was, in fact, correct? As far as I can see in the record, there is no indication that you did so."

Alcock avoided Arbuthnot's piercing gaze. He was right, of course. Not once had Alcock given the Japanese explanation serious consideration, in spite of their many attempts to make him understand, not to mention those of the Dutch letter-writer from Nagasaki.

"Why did the Japanese government issue such a currency? Obviously, to supplement its revenue. It would not have been feasible to slash the silver content by two-thirds all at once. As the minister of foreign affairs informed you, the government gradually reduced the silver content of the ichibu to one-third. Eventually, every time the Japanese government issued one ichibu, it could make a two-ichibu profit. It had done something truly wonderful. It's a story to make the beleaguered financial ministers of Europe green with envy. I have not investigated this, but I believe that the Japanese government has been able to generate an enormous revenue."

Alcock was stunned: he had never foreseen that Arbuthnot would say such things.

"Habit is dangerous, sir. You have often told us that Japanese government officials are incompetent and frequently replaced. Consequently, awareness of what kind of currency they were issuing may have dissipated with each change of regime. Also, the consciousness that they were obtaining an enormous revenue from this source may have dimmed. It must have, or they wouldn't have done anything so stupid as to raise the value of gold, which degraded the currency. By doing so, the government lost all the revenue that it had obtained by issuing ichibus.

"Some people must have been aware, however vaguely, that the ichibu is a currency that actually possesses three times its value in silver content. Accordingly, the claim was asserted on some occasions, and on others retracted."

Alcock wished he could wake up and find that this was only a bad dream. His first thought was to bolt from the office, but he couldn't move: he felt as though he'd been fixed to the spot.

"It's important that you understand *why* the ichibu is actually a currency that can be assigned three times its material worth.

The Japanese government told you that Japan had adopted the gold standard—their gold being in the form of cobangs—and that the ichibu, a silver coin, was an auxiliary currency. They were right, you know.

"In his second letter to you, the minister of foreign affairs stated that five cobangs had the gold content of a twenty-dollar gold piece. The mint later confirmed that statement. Somehow, the Japanese have come to possess a method of accurately analyzing gold content. They found that one cobang is equivalent to four dollars. In the Japanese monetary system, one cobang is worth four ichibu. Consequently, one dollar in Japan is equivalent in value to one ichibu, just as the Japanese claimed. The ichibu is one-third as heavy as the dollar. But even though it weighs only one-third as much, it has the same value. In other words, engraving it with the mint stamp does indeed triple its value."

Alcock was gradually beginning to understand the Japanese currency system. He felt frightfully ill all of a sudden.

"You reported that the ratio of gold to silver in Japan was one to five. That one-to-five ratio, however, was actually that of Japanese gold to silver coin, an auxiliary currency. That ratio was indeed one to five. You seemed amazed that the ratio of gold to silver was so unusually low, but that was nothing to be surprised about."

Alcock realized that Arbuthnot was right.

"You have perhaps heard of Gresham's law: bad money drives out the good. It is a law universally applicable. In this case, the good money is gold coin—the cobang. The bad money is silver coin—the ichibu. Because of Gresham's law, the gold coin was stored away deep in Japanese vaults. Soon after the opening of Yokohama, however, a premium was placed on gold and cobangs came pouring forth."

To Alcock, Arbuthnot had the look of an avenging angel. The man continued relentlessly:

"Think back, if you will, to your first visit to Nagasaki. You reported that the Japanese severely restricted the exchange of currency, that the foreign merchants could not sell their goods, that Japanese goods did not become cheaper in barter trade, and that the Japanese disliked the dollar and would not accept it.

"Let's first consider the restrictions on currency exchange. The original exchange rate was one ichibu to the dollar. It then rose to three ichibus to the dollar. You know what happened, sir. Because foreigners could obtain triple the number of ichibus for their dollars, the prices of all Japanese goods fell to a third of what they had been.

"It may be easier to understand this way: let's say a Japanese merchant has thirty ichibus' worth of goods to sell. Originally, a foreigner would have paid thirty dollars for them. But because of a mistaken exchange rate, he need only pay ten dollars. Did you never once ask yourself, sir, why the prices of goods in Japan were one-third what they were on the China coast?

"The Japanese did not want that exchange rate, but they were pressured into accepting it by the specter of foreign military power, specifically, ours. So they felt that they had no choice but to exchange their money at that rate. Given such circumstances, it was only natural that they would impose severe limits on that exchange."

In his second letter, the minister of foreign affairs had written that if Japan consented to foreign demands, foreigners would be able to buy Japanese goods at one-third their true price. Arbuthnot was saying that the Japanese claim, which the foreign representatives had completely disregarded, was essentially correct.

"The reverse side of that coin was reluctance of the Japanese to buy foreign goods. Initially, the Japanese could buy one dollar's worth of goods for one dollar. But with an exchange rate of three ichibus to the dollar, the Japanese had to spend triple the ichibu to buy one dollar's worth of goods. In other words, an exchange rate of three ichibus to the dollar made foreign goods three times more expensive than they should have been. Again, it was only to be expected that these goods would not sell."

In short, Arbuthnot was saying that the minister of foreign

affairs had been right in claiming that foreign goods had tripled in price for the Japanese.

"This was also why the Japanese were prejudiced against the dollar and would not accept it. At a weight-for-weight exchange rate of three ichibus to the dollar, the Japanese would absorb a three-hundred-percent loss by accepting dollars. They knew this instinctively, even if they couldn't understand the logic behind it. Therefore, they did not like dollars and would not accept them.

"I might remark in passing that, although various factors are responsible for the fall of the dollar against the ichibu, the psychological factor—the Japanese dislike of the dollar—is one that has never changed.

"The weight-for-weight exchange rate is also the reason why Japanese goods did not become cheaper in barter trade. Originally, Japanese goods were not cheap. But because of the absurd weight-for-weight exchange rate, you hastily concluded that Japan had the world's cheapest prices. But as far as I can tell from the documents I have assembled, that was not the case. In fact, prices in Japan were somewhat higher than those in Shanghai and Canton. They did not actually become cheaper, and you should have seen that from the barter trade."

Alcock looked out the window. It had started to rain.

"I would also have you understand that you and the other foreign representatives were employing Japanese labor and buying Japanese goods at one-third their true price. Why didn't you notice that, sir? It strikes me as extremely odd that you wouldn't have. After all, you had numerous opportunities to investigate the matter. You may not like hearing this, but I think you wanted to close your eyes to the fact that if you accepted the Japanese government claims, prices would become significantly higher— in other words, they would return to their rightful level."

Alcock did not flinch at Arbuthnot's harsh words. Everything he was saying might well be correct. Alcock knew that, as far as Harris was concerned, Arbuthnot was right.

"Finally, using the excuse of the palace fire, the Japanese government stopped exchanging ichibus. Any excuse would have done as well. The palace fire simply provided them with the chance they had been waiting for. But then you, in violation of your instructions, which required that you maintain friendly relations, threatened the Japanese with war and forced them to reinstate the false exchange rate. The American minister then pressed them to increase the value of their gold." Alcock recalled that Harris had done so at his urging.

Arbuthnot continued, saying, "Earlier you told me that if the Japanese government had quickly followed your advice to raise the value of gold, cobangs would not have flowed out of the country and confusion could have been avoided. But, as the Japanese soon informed you, if they increased the value of the gold cobang coins—their standard currency—prices would rise accordingly. Because they did not wish that to happen, the Japanese refused to increase the value of gold. And continued to refuse. But when you issued your threats, they suddenly and unaccountably changed their minds and accepted your suggestion. They brought the value of their gold in line with world standards—or more precisely, they raised it 3.375 times. This effectively increased the prices of goods 3.375 times as well.

"I may be mistaken, but I believe that prices in Japan are now rising at an alarming rate. Because no nation can increase prices by 3.375 times all at once, they are no doubt still on the rise. The prices of some goods are rising slowly, others rapidly. All, however, are heading for the 3.375 mark."

The Japanese had often told Alcock that prices were climbing rapidly. But the prices charged by the native agents who frequented the legation had become "special prices," higher than those in the city. Because the Japanese government had urged the agents to charge these exorbitant prices and because Harris had often said that this had been the case since his days in Shimoda, Alcock dismissed the Japanese claim of a "rise in prices" as just another underhanded Oriental tactic. He barely listened, as he felt himself well qualified to assess the truth of the matter. But he was listening now as Arbuthnot explained the reasons for the dangerous inflation. It was all quite simple.

"When prices rise sharply, merchants havve a means of

shifting the burden: they simply increase the prices of goods. But what happens to those who lack that means, the common people and the samurai—the ruling class—whose only income is a fixed stipend, based on a noninflationary economy? They suffer economic hardships as prices mount daily. I believe that few if any Japanese understand the theory behind this inflation, but they know they are being squeezed by it. Where do they direct their anger? At the opening of the country, at trade with foreigners, at a government that would allow such things, and at the treaty nations. This anger, I believe, is closely tied to the indiscriminate killings of foreigners and the fall of one government leader after another."

Alcock found that everything Arbuthnot was saying rang dishearteningly true.

"According to your reports, the Japanese government, which probably should be called the 'Tycoon's government,' rules only part of the country. The mikado, normally a spiritual ruler like the Roman pope, and the *daimyo,* who do not always readily submit to the Tycoon, are also powers in the land. I can well believe that the *daimyo,* who are opposed to the opening of the country and to trade, which they feel have caused the current inflation, would support the mikado and defy the Tycoon's government. And if they do, you foreign representatives—and you alone—will have been responsible for igniting the fires of rebellion."

Alcock was not only persuaded by Arbuthnot's arguments but impressed by the sharpness of his insight.

"As I have already mentioned, the Tycoon's government obtained much of its revenue by issuing ichibus. Raising the value of gold caused that revenue to decline. When the price adjustment process ends—that is, when prices cease rising—the revenue that the government generates by issuing ichibus will completely disappear. Consequently, the Tycoon's government is now badly troubled by a fall in revenue. If some of the *daimyos* support the mikado and defy the Tycoon's government, they will no doubt succeed because it can no longer support itself financially."

Alcock recalled the face of Mizuno, with its staring, double-lidded eyes. It was almost as if he could see that face superimposed over Arbuthnot's.

Alcock had thought that Mizuno was continually throwing up barriers to trade in the form of currency problems. He now realized that, rather than deliberate barriers, they had been unavoidable facts. Alcock, however, had not listened to Mizuno. Instead he had pressured the Bakufu, persuaded the Russian count to do his bidding, driven Mizuno from office, and brought about an increase in the value of gold. The results of his actions were as Arbuthnot had indicated. The truth, Alcock realized, was complex and horrifying.

So that was why Mizuno had had the Japanese mission bring the instructions they did, to secure an agreement from the treaty nations to accept the withdrawal of the ichibu and subsequent recirculation of the notorious nishu.

The instructions might well have been Mizuno's revenge. He must have foreseen this result. Alcock recalled that he had actively lobbied for Mizuno's dismissal.

✳

After Ii's death and the formation of the Kuze-Ando coalition cabinet, Mizuno, who had been demoted to post of *Nishi no Maru Rusui*—Caretaker of the West Keep of the Tycoon's palace—was returned to favor and allowed to serve as diplomatic advisor while retaining his old job. His policies rejected by Harris and Alcock, he had been driven from his post as governor of foreign affairs. Forbidden from appearing openly at negotiations with foreign diplomats, he nevertheless attended, hidden behind a folding screen. He would listen from beginning to end and when necessary, communicate with Ando by written messages. He thus became known as Folding Screen Mizuno.

When the Bakufu sent a mission to Europe to negotiate a delay in the opening of the ports, it tried to dispatch Mizuno as a vice envoy. Actually, Mizuno himself wanted to go in that capacity. Hearing of this, Alcock had strongly objected, as he considered Mizuno to be the "mastermind" behind the Bakufu's financial trickery, and Mizuno was dropped from consideration.

This was not the first time that Mizuno had been prevented from going abroad. When the Japanese mission was dispatched to Washington to exchange ratifications, Iwase, the first treaty negotiator, was selected to head it. But when Iwase was dismissed from his post as commissioner of construction, Mizuno was chosen to take his place. Then the foreign representatives forced Mizuno to step down from his post as governor of foreign affairs, and as a result, he was deprived of the chance to go to Washington.

When the Japanese mission was about to leave for Europe, Mizuno had given them instructions to ask the treaty nations to approve the reissue and recirculation of the nishu. This was after the value of gold had been raised. Mizuno was well aware that reissuing and recirculating the nishu would be technically difficult. But he gave the mission the instructions hoping that, by doing so, he might make the British government reconsider the currency question.

Mizuno realized that even if the British government knew the truth, it might be unable to change anything, but at least he could make them aware that Alcock and Harris had botched things by their willful ignorance. Just as Alcock had suspected, the instructions had been Mizuno's revenge.

※

Alcock stepped out onto the street from his meeting with Arbuthnot. That morning the skies had been clear, but later it started to rain and then snow. On Parliament Street, carriages carrying high government officials and MPs came and went in an endless stream. Leaving the Treasury, Alcock could either turn left toward Trafalgar Square or right toward the Thames. Wanting to avoid the crowds, Alcock turned right.

His mind was still buzzing from the revelations of the meeting.

If he and the other foreign representatives had caused the Yokohama gold rush by not listening to Mizuno, then they were also to blame for trade falling into chaos in the early days of the open ports. In addition, they were responsible for the sudden rise in prices, for inciting the reactionary nationalist factions that opposed the opening of the ports, and for driving the Tycoon's government to the wall and hastening its financial ruin. Yes, it was their responsibility, but the one who had led them was Harris.

Alcock could easily imagine that even prior to the opening of the ports, during his Shimoda days, Harris had been greedily dipping profits from cobangs.

Harris had no doubt soon realized that the ratio of gold to silver in Japan was unusually low. The moment he knew, he should have informed the Japanese and urged them to take countermeasures. But he failed to do so because he was making his fortune from cobangs and didn't want to kill the golden goose.

Alcock now also understood the cause of that strange incident—Heusken's desertion of his post.

He realized that it must have been caused by Heusken's dissatisfaction with his share of the profits in the scheme.

He saw the same cause behind Harris's seclusion and his sudden change of attitude following Heusken's death.

The American government must have learned about Harris's speculations in cobangs, just as it had unmasked similar dealings by the officers of the *Powhatan*. Harris had made a show of becoming intimate with the Japanese government in order to make others believe that his cobangs were gifts from his Japanese friends.

Following the lead of Harris, who had been so eager to speculate in cobangs, Alcock and the other foreign representatives had not listened to the views of the Japanese side. The blame, Alcock told himself, lay entirely with that former supercargo and pseudo-diplomat—Harris.

The foreign merchants in Yokohama, the Dutch doctor in Nagasaki, the *North China Herald,* and the *Hong Kong Press* had all slanderously attacked Alcock only because of the confusion in the currency. The one primarily responsible for creating that confusion had been none other than Harris.

The special ichibu exchange privilege, which had made Alcock a target of censure, would not have been necessary if Harris had not misled him concerning the currency problem. As the leader of the foreign representatives in Japan, Alcock was the only one subjected to this crossfire of criticism. In the foreign settlement of Yokohama, where he should have been treated with the utmost respect, he was instead an object of contempt. He was even barred from entering the foreigners' club. In all the foreign settlements in the Far East, he had never heard of a minister being forbidden to enter the local club.

It was all the fault of one man, who put on a dignified front but was really nothing but a miserly, self-serving tradesman. Alcock was maddened by a surge of anger that he couldn't unleash and a feeling of bitter remorse at his own blindness.

Now that he had learned the truth from Arbuthnot, Alcock focused his attention on a burdensome task that he had to perform immediately: decide what to do about the publication of *The Capital of the Tycoon,* which had already been printed.

The manuscript had reached enormous proportions. Rewriting and reprinting it would be almost impossible. Should he stop publication? That would be regrettable indeed—the book was to redeem him for posterity. Besides, the publisher would never allow it. The only thing to do was to add the new facts he had learned from Arbuthnot.

Alcock had made the last chapter—chapter thirty-nine—his counterattack on the foreign merchants in Yokohama and the newspaper editors in China. Now that he knew the truth, the descriptions in that chapter seemed full of contradictions. He decided to rewrite it, summarizing the currency question.

But to do that would be to completely contradict views he had expressed elsewhere in the book. Alcock decided to close his eyes and present *The Capital of the Tycoon* to the world, contradictions and all.

❋

The Capital of the Tycoon is largely an account of Alcock's experiences in and impressions of Japan. The last chapter—chapter
thirty-nine—begins around the time Alcock left Japan and continues up to his reunion with the Japanese mission in London.
Here, however, he suddenly inserts a discussion of the currency
question:

> The monetary system of the Japanese, conducted on
> restrictive principles, and adapted only to their own use
> when they had no foreign trade or treaties, had been
> shaken to the centre by the American Treaty of 1858,
> negotiated by Mr. Harris, and subsequently copied by all
> the other negotiators. On matters of trade and currency,
> the Japanese could not apparently be so fairly charged with
> ignorance of European practice, as of having simply, in
> their intercourse with the Dutch, sought information to suit
> their own wants.

Harris and Alcock had often agreed with each other that
the Japanese had engaged in barter trade with the Dutch to suit
their own convenience. In his final chapter, however, Alcock
denied this.

> I do not think therefore that when the first discussions took
> place between the Americans on the currency, that the
> charges of ignorance and perversity freely brought against
> them in Hildreth's account of the negotiations were alto-
> gether deserved.

Arbuthnot had traced the course of the Shimoda negotiations by reading and comparing Perry's *Journal* and *Japan As It
Was and Is,* by Richard Hildreth, a noted historian who had
written his book after interviewing members of the Perry expedition. Alcock based this chapter on Arbuthnot's report.

> Indeed the conclusion to which any well-informed
> mind would naturally come, upon careful consideration of

the facts and statements on both sides, would be that the Japanese had the best of the argument; and showed a tolerably correct appreciation of the real question at issue, which was one of vital importance to them in their future relations with Europe. It had been well, perhaps, for them and for us, if the resolution they came to on this occasion had been firmly adhered to, when four years later Mr. Harris was negotiating a new treaty.

The question was no other than this, upon what principle of exchange should American coins be received in payment for goods and supplies? As regarded their relative value with Japanese coins, and the condition of their currency at that particular period, one fact appears to have been known to both parties, namely, that silver coins were over-valued in relation both to the gold and copper money. When an endeavour was made therefore by the Representative of the United States to obtain a recognition of the Mexican dollar as of equal nominal value with the silver coin of Japan, the Japanese governors insisted that the foreign coin was but bullion to them, while the American Finance Commissioners—nominated by Commodore Perry from among his pursers to discuss the question—contended the effect of this would be to put their silver dollar, so far as payments in Japan were concerned, on a level with the silver itziboo [ichibu], which weighed only one-third as much. But if the relative value of their silver and gold coins was (as we know it to have been) in that proportion, the Japanese were perfectly justified in objecting to the dollar being circulated with equivalent weights of itziboos [ichibus]. No inquiry appears to have been made regarding the relation which the silver coins of Japan bore to their gold and copper, yet this was essential to any equitable arrangement, and lay at the root of the whole matter in question.

Mizuno had proposed investigating the value of coins in China and tried to persuade Alcock and Harris to reconsider the Japanese currency question. Like Harris, Alcock had ignored Mizuno. Secretly he was thoroughly ashamed of himself, but—feigning ignorance—he presented Arbuthnot's views as though they were his own.

Anyone interested in currency and economics, and capable of simple rational deduction would have found this section of *The Capital of the Tycoon* somewhat strange. Doubt would give way to certainty if reference is made to the early chapters. For example, chapter six contained the following passage:

> There have not been wanting Europeans (chiefly visitors) and some among the Dutch residents, I think,—who have contended that the Japanese were right in considering the itziboo [ichibu] as a mere "bank token," having a money value far above its real worth, as so much silver,—and that to hold them to the exact terms of the American and subsequent treaties, bound to give weight for weight of the then existing silver coins, for European coins,—was to inflict upon them a wrong and loss. But without going into the different theories of a currency, it seemed to me then, as it does still, that there was a ready method of testing the truth or fallacy of the Japanese argument.

One of the questions dealt with by the "different theories of a currency" was that of the relationship between Japanese silver and gold coins. In chapter six, Alcock says that he did not address this question himself, but in chapter thirty-nine he scolds the Americans for not doing so either. This section of chapter six continues as follows:

> I suggested to them at once an effective remedy, by lowering the relative mint value of their gold and silver coinage, increasing the value of the former from four itziboos [ichibus] to twelve or thirteen, bringing it sufficiently close to the average rates in Europe to secure them from any operation for the export of gold. Unfortunately, I think, they hesitated. . . . Ultimately, as will be seen, they altered their gold coinage to the European standard, but too late to prevent large exportation and much mischief.

The contradictions in these passages bothered Alcock. Even so, he could not very well go back and rewrite chapter six, so he ignored them.

Alcock also wrote, "One error begets another—one false step is the parent of many."

As a result of his own errors, Alcock had strongly opposed the foreign merchants in Yokohama. In chapter thirty-nine, Alcock addressed those merchants as follows:

> If the Foreign Powers, in the treaties of 1858, have been mistaken in imposing upon Japan an engagement for the exchange and circulation of foreign coins, which is anomalous as regards international principles of intercourse between European Powers, and in its essence erroneous and vicious; the sooner it is departed from the better, even at some risk of monetary derangement and great embarrassment to commerce in those regions.

The article providing for the weight-for-weight exchange of currency was in effect for only one year. But even after that year, foreign merchants in Yokohama—hard hit by the decline of the dollar against the ichibu—persistently demanded that foreign representatives press for the continued implementation of the weight-for-weight exchange article. In this section, Alcock said that because the article was anomalous and mistaken, he could not force the Japanese to implement it.

But the chief spreader of error had been Harris, without question. Harris had misrepresented everything. Alcock carefully turned his guns on the American minister:

> I believe the two greatest and most generally pervading causes of hostility are to be traced to the feudal element and the monetary perturbation reacting especially upon the military retainers and official classes, and giving them an additional and special motive of hostility. They believe the whole nation has suffered a wrong and injury by Mr. Harris's original clause in the American Treaty, stipulating that American coin (and therefore in sequel all foreign coins, more especially the Mexican dollar) should pass current for the corresponding weight in Japanese coin of the same description.

Alcock had never known this while in Japan: he owed this insight to Arbuthnot.

"I am not aware what motives may have led Mr. Harris to propose [this]."

Alcock understood very well what those motives had been, but he did not have any proof. Now that he thought of it, he regretted that he hadn't pressed Moriyama harder for the truth about Mr. Harris.

> . . . and it is still less easy to conceive what possible induce-
> ment the Japanese could have had for yielding consent, to
> a proposition which they had four years before resolutely
> and consistently refused to accede to, when proposed by
> Commodore Perry. No inquiry appears to have been made
> as to the effects of the well-known relation which the silver
> coins of Japan bore to their gold and copper coins, on
> nominal prices.

Harris *had* made no inquiries, but neither, for that matter, had Alcock. Closing his eyes to his own failings, Alcock contin-ued: "Whether the Japanese negotiators were clear-sighted enough or sufficiently well-informed, to duly estimate and fore-see the exact influence and degree of perturbation such an engagement as the clause in question involved, may be ques-tioned."

During his negotiations with Harris, Iwase had shown a clear understanding of the article in question.

> Seeing, however, that four years before the whole subject
> had been maturely discussed; and that the Japanese Gov-
> ernors had said, that "the Mexican dollar was but bullion to
> them," and thus "hit with precision the point at issue," as
> has been well observed by an impartial authority in financial
> matters in this country, I cannot but conclude that they did
> not enter into the engagement blindfolded, or fall into a
> trap, as by some has been supposed.

Although Alcock never alludes to Arbuthnot by name, surely he must be the "impartial authority" that he mentions in this paragraph.

It must be abundantly evident, therefore, that whatever be the true history of the negotiations which took place with Mr. Harris; or the motives by which the American negotiator was induced to impose so unprecedented or anomalous an engagement, and the Japanese to accede to it—the latter signed under a mental reservation to alter their silver currency in the way they subsequently attempted by reducing it as much as they deemed it overrated, that is two-thirds—issuing a coinage of half itziboos [ichibus], two of which should contain the same weight of silver as three of the then current itziboos [ichibus].

In other words, the Japanese had issued the nishu.

That Mr. Harris had not contemplated this as one of the contracting parties is to be inferred by his joining of the other Foreign Representatives in resisting the change [The "other Foreign Representatives," of course, included Alcock himself.] . . . at all events until further discussion and a reference to our respective Governments should give time to clear the question of all doubt and obscurity.

Alcock is guilty of a slight dissimulation here: neither Harris nor Alcock had referred this question to his home government. Without understanding Mizuno's intentions, Alcock had simply sent all the relevant documents to the Treasury. He did not mention this, however. Instead, he implicitly criticized Harris as a fool who did not realize the true nature of the problem to the very end.

Alcock next undertook a lengthy defense of the special ichibu exchange privilege that he had obtained for foreign representatives, including, of course, himself.

I have been induced to enter more fully into the details than I should have otherwise deemed necessary for the general reader, because I find occasion has been taken since my departure from Japan, to make them the subject of a series of scurrilous attacks in the local papers.

Although the attacks had begun long before, they had escalated as Alcock had prepared to return home. By entering "more fully into the details," Alcock was able to direct a counter blow at the foreign merchants in Yokohama: one of his original purposes in writing the book.

> As for the grasping after pecuniary advantages implied in all these imputations, the calumny is pointless against a public servant who, after more than twenty years of arduous service, chiefly in the East, returns poorer than when he first entered. But to resume the consideration of the general question of the currency, thus temporarily in abeyance . . .

Alcock returned the discussion to its original theme.

Now that he reflected on it, Alcock was vexed to have been squelched so thoroughly by Arbuthnot. A financier in Europe (Arbuthnot) and a diplomatic agent in Japan (Alcock) would naturally approach the subject from two very different points. He thus tried to rationalize his actions with reasons that were not quite rational. He had been mistaken, he wanted to say, but he couldn't have done otherwise. "So sudden and violent a rending of the monetary arrangements of a country produced by the interference of foreigners, is without precedent in modern times."

It was impossible to find a precedent not only in modern times but throughout history, anywhere in the world. "Depreciation of currency in other countries, however rapid, has generally been foreshadowed and sufficiently gradual to admit of a progressive readjustment of prices, and to a certain extent of contracts."

A 337.5 percent rise in the value of gold had brought about a corresponding increase in the prices of goods. Alcock, however, advanced his argument from the opposite standpoint—that of the ichibu, the key currency that had fallen to 1/3.375 of its former value. The difference was one of perspective: whether one examined the question from the front or the rear. But the facts or phenomena observed did not differ in the slightest. "But in the case of Japan the value of the current money was at once reduced to one-third of its former rate, by external pressure, and for the advantage of foreign merchants."

It had not been done "for the advantage of foreign merchants" but because of "external pressure." In other words, pressure from Alcock and Harris had caused the value of the current money—the ichibu—to fall to one-third its former rate in relation to gold bullion. On the other hand, the prices of goods had tripled. Up to this point, Alcock had vigorously defended himself. He had also been playing with words. But when he took up his pen again, his anger at Harris came out with a vengeance. "It is beyond all doubt under these circumstances that the inconvenience occasioned by the consequent derangement of money prices and of contracts expressed in money must have been immense."

Just that sort of "inconvenience" was to be experienced in Germany after World War I and in Japan after World War II. This was caused by 100 marks (or yen) on a given day being valued at less than that 100 marks the next day. Alcock was right: the country was suffering from rampant inflation.

"In one respect, moreover, the disturbance of wages had no less manifestly a political bearing, which may, or rather which must, seriously affect our future relations with the Japanese."

Alcock proceeded to go into detail:

> The Daimyos have in their service large bodies of retainers who in addition to their food and clothing receive a very small allowance paid in itziboos [ichibus]. This, barely sufficient before to enable them to dress themselves and support their families, by the depreciation of the currency became altogether inadequate. The discontent and irritation caused in the mind of this class is intense, as we have evidence written in blood. The Daimyos, whose pecuniary interests have probably been little benefited by foreign trade, owing to the profits of the sale of all produce being

intercepted by the Tycoon's officials at the consular ports; and who are alarmed and exasperated by the danger these foreign relations bring to their feudal privileges and rights, and the institutions of the country generally, have obviously no motive if they had the means of allaying this discontent by increasing the money-wages of their retainers. On the contrary, there is very little doubt they have profited by the circumstances to incense their followers more against foreigners.

Here it is necessary to briefly explain the situation in Japan at the time.

The Bakufu issued not only the ichibu but several other types of substitute currency as well. The purpose of issuing these currencies was to generate revenue. Surviving records indicate that in the four decades before the opening of Japanese ports under the Harris treaty, the Bakufu obtained forty percent of its revenue in this way.

But because the Bakufu issued these currencies so adroitly and managed its gold and silver bullion so well, and because its officials came and went with such rapidity, even Treasury officials—with the exception of a small low ranking handful for got that the ichibu was a stand-in currency.

When Perry arrived, the Japanese supplied his ships with wood, water, food, and coal. The Japanese negotiating the treaty with the Perry expedition knew that they had to be paid for these supplies, but how? How should they value the ichibu and the Mexican dollar, which were both silver? In other words, how were they to set the exchange rate between the two currencies?

They thought that a weight-for-weight exchange would be strange somehow, but they didn't know exactly why. A few low-ranking officials knew, but the negotiators didn't know that they knew. Instead, they contacted trade officials in Nagasaki, the only place in Japan where trade with foreigners was conducted.

From Nagasaki they got the following reply: the ichibu, said the Nagasaki officials, was a currency given its value by a government stamp. The Mexican dollar, however, was simply silver bullion, valued according to its silver content. Therefore, it was impossible to compare them by weight. The Mexican dollar weighed three times as much as the ichibu. But the ichibu had been given triple the value of its silver by the government stamp. Consequently, they were equal in value.

The Japanese negotiating the treaty with the Perry expedition did not correctly understand this reply from Nagasaki. Instead, they simply repeated it to Perry's negotiators, like so many parrots. Then, trained to obedience rather than decision making, they stubbornly refused to budge.

Their strange attitude excited the suspicions of Perry's negotiators, but they consented to the Japanese demands and reported them to the American government, as Harris had told Alcock. Hildreth had described this in his account of the negotiations, and Alcock recorded it in his book. As a result, the United States government sent Harris to Japan, charging him with the task of "settling the currency question."

Soon after landing in Shimoda, Harris proceeded to do just that. Harris negotiated with the local authorities in Shimoda and with Iwase, who happened to be there on a visit from Edo.

After examining the records of the negotiations with the Perry expedition, which had been left behind at Shimoda, Iwase and others on the Japanese side began negotiating with Harris. But Iwase and the others imprudently believed Harris's claims to be correct and their own, mistaken.

Ever since Perry's arrival in Japan, Japanese negotiators had thought nothing of lying to advance their own interests. Iwase and the others thus assumed that their countrymen's claims were strategic fabrications. Without conducting their own independent investigation, they accepted Harris's demand for the exchange of currency on a weight-for-weight basis and incorporated it into the Convention of Shimoda, which did not require ratification.

Later, Iwase, together with Mizuno, went to Nagasaki to conclude supplementary treaties to the treaties of amity and friendship with Holland and Russia. In the course of the negotiations, the Nagasaki officials who were helping them draft the treaties told them that the ichibu should be considered a paper like currency. Iwase and Mizuno thus became aware of the true nature of the ichibu.

Later, the Bakufu began negotiating a commercial treaty with Harris.

On returning from Nagasaki, Mizuno opposed these negotiations, saying that there was no reason to hurry. Hotta, the Prince of Sakura, who was then serving as prime minister and minister of foreign affairs, demoted Mizuno and put Iwase in charge of the negotiations with Harris.

Iwase also knew the true situation regarding the ichibu. Even so, he included a provision for the exchange of currency of equal type and equal weight in Article V of the Treaty of Edo. Why? Because Hotta—a member of the extreme progressive faction—was sensitive to foreign pressure.

Hotta did not know that England intended to be "an innocent virgin" in its dealings with Japan. The Japanese negotiators feared that fierce, warlike England would treat Japan as unjustly as it had China.

It is no wonder that Hotta, based on what he was able to infer about the British from their attitude toward China, should fear England. He therefore hurried treaty negotiations with Harris to provide a shield against England as quickly as possible.

Harris in turn hastened the negotiations so that he would have the honor of being the first to conclude a commercial treaty with Japan. Hotta also had a similar motive for expediting the negotiations with Harris.

What would have happened if the Japanese had told Harris the truth about the currency situation in Japan and convinced him that the ichibu was like a paper currency?

Using the weight-for-weight exchange rate, Harris was able to buy Japanese goods, hire Japanese servants, enjoy Kichi's company, and obtain cobangs and foreign gold coins, all at one-third the rightful charges. Treating the ichibu like a paper currency would have meant recalculating everything. Before doing that, Harris would undoubtedly have scuttled the treaty negotiations.

That would have been a blow to Hotta, who saw no alternative to hastening the negotiations. Hotta thus persuaded Iwase to accept the inevitable and include Article V, which provided for the weight-for-weight exchange of similar types of currencies, as Harris had demanded.

Hotta planned to correct the problem later by issuing a coin like the nishu for use only in the treaty ports. Sometime after the signing of the treaty and before the opening of the ports, he also intended to tell Harris the facts about the currency situation in Japan, including his plan to issue a new coin. Of course, he would close his eyes to any profiteering by Harris. . . .

After the treaty was signed, however, a new government came in, and both Hotta and Iwase fell from power. All that remained was Article V.

After Hotta's fall, Mizuno—who had also been shunted aside—was reinstated as a governor of foreign affairs. Understanding the meaning of Article V, Mizuno issued the nishu in accordance with the article and confronted the foreign representatives over the currency question.

Just as Alcock wrote, Japan "did not enter into the engagement blindfolded, or fall into a trap, as by some has been supposed." On the other hand, Harris "had not contemplated this [issuing of the nishu] as one of the contracting parties. . . ." The American minister resisted contemplating the currency situation, not only when he signed the treaty but throughout his stay in Japan.

While still a supercargo, Harris had done business in South China and was thoroughly conversant with the prices of labor and goods on the China coast. Although prices in Japan were somewhat higher, they were not all that different. Then he came to Japan and, forcing the Japanese to accept a false exchange rate, caused the prices of Japanese goods and services to decline to one-third of their former level. In short, prices in Japan fell absurdly low: one-third of what they were in China.

Anyone with ordinary common sense would have wondered why the prices of goods and services were so low in Japan. They would also have at least considered the Japanese claim that the ichibu's value had been tripled by a government stamp and was thus equivalent to that of the Mexican dollar, which was three times its weight. The Japanese had first made this claim to the Perry expedition and had stubbornly continued to assert it. They had also said the same thing to Harris. If they were correct, a weight-for-weight exchange rate would enable foreigners to buy Japanese goods and hire Japanese labor at one-third their true price. Everything would thus become ridiculously cheap.

If Harris had pursued this line of thought, he might have quickly arrived at a correct understanding of the currency situation. But doubts about the rightness of his own opinions never occurred to Harris. If they had, his profit margin might have suffered.

Harris first became aware of the truth about the currency situation in Japan when he read chapter thirty-nine of Alcock's *The Capital of the Tycoon.*

The price rises of this period might be called the Harris Shock Inflation. The Harris Shock Inflation was a 337.5 percent increase in prices. This explosive hike caused a near panic.

At this time, Japanese society was divided into four classes: the samurai, farmers, craftsmen, and merchants, in descending order. But among the common people, which included the lower three groups, clear-cut class distinctions did not exist. A distinction was generally drawn only between samurai and nonsamurai commoners.

The samurai and commoners hardest hit by the Harris Shock Inflation were the ones who had no means of increasing the income they received for their goods or services. The samurai who lived on fixed stipends belonged in this category. Skyrocketing prices brought about a sharp drop in the buying power of their wages, which they were powerless to prevent. The greatest victims of inflation were thus the samurai, who also happened to be the only Japanese to carry arms.

They did not understand the real cause of their distress, but they did know that trade with foreigners and the opening of the country were somehow to blame.

The barbarians were importing uselss luxuries while making off with the goods they needed for daily life. They were causing prices to rise and the standard of living to fall. They were robbing the country blind. They reasoned that opening Japan to the barbarians and trading with them had brought about this calamity and it was the Bakufu that had permitted both.

The hard-pressed samurai vented their anger and frustration at the Bakufu. They also found another outlet: murdering foreigners.

The *ronin,* masterless samurai, suffered even more than the employed samurai. The *ronin* had no steady income. But prices continued their relentless climb, day after day. And day after day, as their economic survival became more uncertain, their anger grew. The *ronin* blamed the same villains that other samurai held responsible for their woes: the Bakufu, trade with foreigners, and the opening of the country. The *ronin,* however, were more straightforward. They directed their anger at the merchants.

"Those who give valuable goods to the barbarians, cause prices to rise, afflict the people and commit other despicable acts shall suffer the punishment of heaven," read one of the notices posted by the *ronin.* Appointing themselves the agents of heaven, the *ronin* began by committing robberies. The common people, however, found little comfort in such lawless acts.

The political forces centering around the emperor, in Kyoto, who had himself become politically conscious, adopted *joi* ("expel the barbarian") as their rallying cry. The oppression of the Ii regime caused this *joi* fever to rage even more furiously. The sharp rise in prices—and the consequent panic—occurred mainly in places that functioned on a money economy: Edo, Osaka, Kyoto, and the provincial cities. Steadily, inexorably, inflation spread throughout the country. As the samurai and *ronin* became more politically conscious, they naturally began to oppose the Bakufu and its policy of opening the country and permitting trade. They started to advocate expelling the barbarians and overthrowing the Bakufu.

If Harris and Alcock had understood the true nature of the

problem and had not tried to mislead the Japanese, if they had lent an ear to Mizuno's repeated explanations and had opened the country and begun trade properly, without creating economic distortions, runaway inflation could have been avoided and the Bakufu could have become steadily richer from customs revenues. It could then have used its financial power to win an easy victory over the *joi* forces centered in Kyoto. Leaving aside the question of whether this victory would have ultimately been good or bad, it might have strengthened the Bakufu's system of administration—and prevented the chaos that later swept the country.

The Japanese are a practical people, astonishingly quick to change and yet retain their identity.

They might have realized that opening the country to foreigners and trading with them had certain advantages after all. Once this mood had spread, it might have been possible to halt the trend favoring the anti-Bakufu forces. Everything might have then moved in a different direction.

But by raising the value of cobangs, the Bakufu lost a source of revenue that accounted for forty percent of its income. As a result, it became too fiscally weak to cross swords with the opposition.

Alcock reflected on the implications of Arbuthnot's dismaying revelations. He was ashamed of his own obtuseness. How could he have been so blind? True, he had taken up a post in a country about which he had known virtually nothing, but that did not excuse his blunders, his inability to see what should have been as plain as the nose on his face.

But he consoled himself with the thought that Harris, not he, had made the first, wrong judgments. Harris, not he, had let greed overcome all other considerations. He and the others had merely followed Harris's lead. He felt certain that chapter thirty-nine would vindicate his behavior in the eyes of the public—and strike a crushing blow against his enemies.

Yes, most decidedly, Harris had been the source of all his woes.

Fortunately, Alcock was not an introspective sort; he did not torment himself with the question of why he had let himself be led by a man whose understanding was so shallow—and whose motives were so suspect.

8

The
Final Chapter

Together with his new wife, Alcock returned to Japan in 1864, one year after the publication of *The Capital of the Tycoon*. While in England, he had been awarded the First Order of Bath and a knighthood. Alcock had also been given the authority to employ military force when the situation required it.

He arrived in Nagasaki on March 2. A reporter from the *Illustrated London News* who happened to be in the city interviewed Alcock and asked him what his policy toward Japan would be now that he was once again British representative.

Alcock's dyspeptic countenance looked even grimmer than usual. Making a stern face, offset by his acerbic smile, Alcock answered: "There is no need to employ military force to gain the respect and trust of the Japanese government and people."

The phrase "the logic of the sword" had been Alcock's byword in Asian diplomacy. But even though now he had been given the authority to use military force when the situation demanded it, he told the *Illustrated London News* reporter that such force would be unnecessary. Alcock's stance toward Japan had evidently undergone an about-face.

The Capital of the Tycoon was sent to Yokohama, where it was circulated among the foreign merchants. The attacks that Alcock had scattered throughout the book further hardened them against him. Alcock's feelings toward the Tycoon's government had changed, but his confrontational stance toward the foreign merchants in Yokohama had not. Once again, Alcock had placed himself in a very uncomfortable position.

Alcock had done something to make that position even more uncomfortable. The protocol that he and the other foreign representatives had negotiated with the Bakufu regarding the special ichibu exchange privilege stated that officers aboard visiting warships could change three dollars and seamen one dollar a day at government offices in each treaty port.

An exchange limit of three dollars a day for officers and one dollar for seamen would not have amounted to much if they were in port only a short while. But if their stay were a long one, as it often was, this limit would quickly take on a new meaning.

British and French troops had been stationed in Yokohama beginning in June 1863 to protect the city. The British troops included the 20th Infantry, which had just arrived from Hong Kong. The Japanese in Yokohama dubbed the 20th the "To-wante" (the Japanese pronunciation of "twenty") or the "Red Army" because of their red uniforms. The officers and men of the Red Army, as well as the French troops stationed in Yoko-hama, were all permitted this special exchange privilege.

At this time $100 was worth anywhere from 225 to 235 ichibus. The marines were allowed to exchange one dollar a day, or thirty dollars a month. Exercising this privilege, they would change their dollars for ichibus at the Government Exchange House and then take the ichibus to money changers in the city, where they would sell them. When the rate in the city was 235 ichibus, they could make a profit of $8.30 a month. When it was 225, they could make $10. This was nearly the equivalent of a marine's monthly pay. The officers made three times as much, from $25 to $30.

On January 1, 1864, three months before Alcock was again posted to Japan, the *Japan Commercial News* ran the following letter in its New Year's Day edition:

> Last but not least, let us pass in review the Cur-
> rency Question, premising that we, like the true sailor,
> go for

Three ichibus to the dollar,
and the sill'er for ever

We truly confess that we would like to get as much
of the Tycoon's money in exchange for our dollars as
the Admirals and their men or the Ministers and their
Consuls. How often have we watched those stout,
strong and hearty seamen during the dog-days of
Yokohama staggering, yes, literally staggering, under
their loads of dollars, with the trim and sprightly
pursers hard-bye, wending their way by the shortest
of Cuts to the Treasury Department of the local
Custom House; there to tell out their thousands of
dollars, while a triple return in Ichiboos is being got
ready by the hard-worked officials. Talk of the glori-
ous days of '59! Why, Mr. Alcock's virtuous indignation would pale before the capacious appetite of the
Hearts of Oak in the piping times of '63! No part of
their duty is more punctually and scrupulously per-
formed than this labor of love by our stead-fast de-
fenders.

The Red Army was stationed on the Yokohama Bluff. Today
it is nothing but a dreary jumble of warehouses, but then it
offered a wonderful view. As the popular song went, "Hama
Park, with its view of the harbor."

From there the "stout and hearty seamen" and pursers
would cross Yatobashi Bridge and walk along the Bund to the
tax office. Because the seamen were staggering under heavy
loads of dollars, they were evidently not exchanging their personal money but that of their entire regiments. The foreign
merchants in Yokohama viewed this spectacle with disgust. This
would never have happened, they felt, if Alcock had not concluded that absurd protocol with the Japanese. The foreign
merchants in Yokohama had never been able to forget—or
forgive—Alcock's many assaults on their dignity.

The writer signed his name as Commerce, Credit and Cash,
a name which recalled the aliases that had been used in requesting ichibus. His letter, however, expressed the sentiments of

many of the foreign merchants who had lived in Yokohama since the opening of the ports. The editors decided to run it on New Year's Day, the day Alcock was scheduled to resume his post.

In a book titled *Young Japan,* J. R. Black, a Yokohama newspaper reporter, commented that "by boo [ichibu] exchange a soldier's [or a sailor's] pay was actually nearly doubled."

That was in fact the case.

> But where was a private soldier to get a dollar a day to exchange? Well! there was no difficulty of that kind experienced. It was all managed through the paymaster. The money was found—the exchange was taken: but he got the amount of his pay—and, in the first instance, that only, in native currency at the exchange of three boos for one dollar; the rest all went into what was called an "Ichibu fund."

In other words, they would save the amount that they made by exchanging ichibus in the form of an ichibu fund.

> On the 20th Regiment arriving here, the amount over and above the exchange on the true pay, accumulated so fast, and to such an amount, that a meeting of the officers was convened, and it was decided to establish a general fund: from which, first, the exchange on the full pay of all the officers receiving over three dollars a day should be made up, and then, the balance should be divided between the officers and men in shares proportionate to their pay, the soldier getting one share, a captain about thirty, and major about fifty-three shares and so on.

If these figures are correct, the officers were extracting a fairly substantial profit from the earnings of the soldiers and sailors. For the French and English officers, Japan was wonderful duty, just as it was for the diplomats stationed there.

On resuming his post, Alcock noticed the strange way the

Red Army was growing steadily richer. He also saw the letter in the *Japan Commercial News.*

Of course, Alcock had not requested the special diplomatic privilege, which permitted the exchange of $100 for 300 ichibus, for that purpose. But his original intent had unexpectedly become completely distorted. Alcock once again found himself the object of harsh enmity.

✳

When Alcock arrived back in Yokohama, trade was nearly at a standstill, largely because the Bakufu had suppressed the export of what was nearly Japan's only export commodity: raw silk thread.

Under pressure from the *joi* faction, the Bakufu had sent another diplomatic mission to Europe to negotiate the closing of Yokohama, but this was, as the mission eventually discovered, an impossible task. To effect that closing, the Bakufu interfered with the export of silk. Merchants in the Japanese section of Yokohama gradually shuttered their shops, giving the boom-town a deserted look.

Trade in Nagasaki was also nearly paralyzed because the Choshu clan the leader of the *joi* faction—had blockaded the Shimonoseki Straits, between the main island of Honshu and Kyushu. Goods from western and northern Japan, including Hokkaido, were brought to Osaka by ship. From there they were distributed to other regions of the nation. Except for marine products, nearly all goods exported from Nagasaki came from Osaka. Also, nearly all imported goods were sent to Osaka. Given this pattern of distribution, the blockade of the Shimono-seki Straits effectively halted the flow of imports from and exports to Nagasaki. The stoppage of trade made the lights go out in Nagasaki as well.

On arriving at his post, Alcock quickly began to analyze the situation and collect new information. He soon decided boldly on military action. The four treaty powers—Britain, France, the United States, and Holland—assembled an allied squadron that delivered a crushing blow to the Choshu clan.

Although he had been given the authority to employ military force, Alcock had denied the need for wielding such power when he first returned to Japan. But he could not tolerate the continued paralysis of trade. Also, although he had changed his position toward the Tycoon's government, its repeated duplicity and delays made him revert to his original stance. Finally, it appeared that the *joi* faction would stop at nothing. These factors made Alcock decide on military action.

Alcock hoped that a display of military power would bring pressure to bear on the elements around the emperor that still opposed the treaties and make them accept ratification. In the end, Alcock embarked on military action against the Choshu clan because he took a favorable view of the Bakufu's prospects. He thought that such action might force the Bakufu, the mikado, and the anti-Bakufu *daimyo* to somehow build a new political system that would support the treaties.

It was the Bakufu that had exchanged articles of ratification with the treaty nations. Ever since Tokugawa Ieyasu had seized political power in 1603, the Bakufu had enjoyed the exclusive authority to conduct diplomatic relations and manage domestic affairs. It had signed the treaties independently. Naturally, it had had no problems in ratifying them.

But the various changes in the political situation arising from the ratification of the treaties, as well as the growing social unrest caused by the steep inflation following the opening of the country, had strengthened the mikado's newfound political influence. The mikado's imperial sanction had thus come to have the same political significance as ratificaton by the Bakufu. This was true internationally as well as domestically. As far as Alcock and the other foreign representatives were concerned, the treaties had been duly ratified by the Tycoon's government, but they had not been ratified by the mikado who, like the Roman pope, was a political fifth wheel. It was a confusing situation indeed.

The contest at Shimonoseki resulted in an overwhelming victory for the allied European forces. Choshu ended its blockade of the straits and trade in Nagasaki once again began to flourish. The Tycoon's government stopped interfering with silk exports, and trade in Yokohama immediately recommenced to boom.

Soon after, Alcock was ordered home. This recall order amounted to a near dismissal. The home government did not know that Alcock had employed military force. It had recalled him out of concern that he *might* use such force: he had hinted as much in his official dispatches.

When it was learned that an order had arrived recalling Alcock, there was a sudden outpouring of praise for him in Yokohama. J. S. Gow, who had succeeded Keswick at Jardine, Matheson, and Charles Rickerby, the manager of the Yokohama Branch of the Central Bank of Western India, applauded his resolute determination and many achievements and expressed their regret at his departure.

Both Gow and Rickerby had first come to Yokohama in the spring of 1862. They felt differently toward Alcock than did the old-time residents, who continued to view him with cold disdain. Even so, Alcock left for home cheered by the hymns of praise that had burst forth from at least certain of Yokohama's citizens.

In a sense, chapter thirty-nine of *The Capital of the Tycoon* was a gamble. Although Alcock did not say so anywhere in this chapter, he effectively disowned all of his words and deeds since arriving in Yokohama and admitted all of his past errors. He thus exposed himself to another thrashing by his enemies. In chapter thirty-nine, Alcock also expressed his concern that "this question of currency . . . would inevitably react upon our future relations with the country and its Government." This indicates that he was also worried about a possible reaction from the Japanese government.

Even so, Alcock struck a defiant pose: he didn't really care whether his fears came to pass. In any event, he would stand his ground. After admitting his errors, he would try to argue his case with the foreign merchants and the Japanese government. Toward the Japanese government, this would take the form of an almost abject apology—he had resigned himself to that. But, none of these fears in the end materialized. The foreign merchants continued to criticize the special ichibu exchange privilege, but neither the merchants nor the Bakufu reacted to anything Alcock had written in chapter thirty-nine.

This was not quite what he had expected. But he did not consider it his responsibility to advertise his own faults. None of this, he thought, should have been a surprise: people are basically not very interested in currency and economics. He tried to forget all about the issues raised in chapter thirty-nine. But there was one person that he could not forget: Mizuno.

From time to time, Alcock wondered what Mizuno was doing and how he regarded Harris and himself. He often felt a strong desire to meet Mizuno again. But Alcock restrained himself: even if he did meet him, nothing could come of it. He couldn't undo what had been done.

An order from the Home Government passed Alcock on his way back to England: it expressed general understanding of his later dispatches and approval of his actions. Alcock returned home a disappointed man, but the next year he was promoted to envoy extraordinary and minister plenipotentiary to China and once again left for Asia.

Three years later, at the end of 1867, the *daimyos* and chief retainers of the Choshu and Satsuma clans, together with the rest of the opposition forces, overthrew the Bakufu, and with Emperor Meiji, who had succeeded Emperor Komei, at their head, established a new government. Alcock heard the news in China.

Alcock resigned as minister to China and ended his diplomatic career in 1871. He continued to be brilliantly active in many areas: as chairman of the board of Westminster Hospital, founder of the Victoria Jubilee Institute for Nurses, president of the Royal Geographical Society, chairman of the African Exploration Fund, British Commissioner to the Paris Exposition of 1878, and founder of the British North Borneo Company.

When he heard of Alcock's doings across the Atlantic, Harris realized again the size of the gap that had opened between him and his former colleague.

✳

Unlike Alcock, Harris had not kept a journal for a book about Japan. But on leaving Penang for the United States in May 1855, he had begun writing a journal to aid him in his job-seeking campaign.

Later, when the investigation into the cobang profiteering of the *Powhatan*'s officers exposed his own speculations, Harris wisely abandoned the idea of publishing this record of his personal experiences.

Harris saw Alcock's *The Capital of the Tycoon,* which was also published in New York, in the spring of 1863, more than one year after he had left Japan.

Leafing through *The Capital of the Tycoon,* Harris once again felt the urge to write a book about his experiences in Japan. After all, it was he who had concluded the first commercial treaty. He was fully qualified to publish such a book.

But when he glanced at the last chapter, chapter thirty-nine, he realized that Alcock had completely disowned Harris's actions. "I cannot but conclude that they did not enter into the engagement blindfolded, or fall into a trap, as by some has been supposed." Alcock was branding him a thief. In truth, his actions in Japan had made it hard for him to vindicate himself from such charges. Once again, Harris reconsidered his decision to write a book.

Harris lived a long life. He died on February 15, 1878, fifteen years after he had left Japan. Nothing came of his plan to publish a volume of reminiscences about Japan.

Harris, a life-long bachelor, willed his estate to his niece, a Miss Bessie A. Harris. Included in that estate was a journal, the existence of which Harris had completely forgotten in his later years.

Miss Harris, who had never married, had little to occupy her time. She read her uncle's journal again and again, and as she read, began to think of showing it to the world.

But starting just before the signing of the treaty, her uncle's diary was filled with passages that she was certain would not be suitable for publication. These passages described such embarrassing episodes as his relations with women and his quarrel with Heusken. She decided to abandon her project of publishing a volume describing the signing of the treaty, her uncle's greatest achievement.

Her uncle's estate also included a copy of *The Capital of the*

Tycoon, by Mr. Alcock, his old colleague. She read this book as well. *The Capital of the Tycoon* mercilessly heaped scorn on the actions that her uncle had described in his journal after being permanently stationed in Edo as the American minister. She realized that she could not publish a volume covering events after the opening of the ports, either.

Finally, after careful study, she decided that it would be better to suppress all entries after February 27, 1858. Acting on that decision, Miss Bessie proceeded to burn all volumes of the journal after that date. She then took the remaining material, dated up to February 27, to Dr. William Elliot Griffis.

In his preface to the 1930 edition, Dr. Mario E. Cosenza wrote: "The earlier portion of Mr. Harris's *Journal* (which includes his mission to Siam, and which is approximately one-third of the entire manuscript) is here published for the first time. The portion of the *Journal* relating to Japan was published (with omissions) in 1895 by Dr. William Elliot Griffis in his book *Townsend Harris, First American Envoy to Japan*."

The journal thus appeared eighteen years after Harris's death. Alcock died two years later, in 1897.

Miss Harris lived a long life. Her selection from her uncle's journal excited little notice and finally went out of print. Thirty-nine years later she brought her uncle's papers to Dr. Mario E. Cosenza, the director of Townsend Harris Hall, the Preparatory High School of The College of the City of New York, which Harris had helped found. In 1930, Cosenza published the journal under the misleading title *The Complete Journal of Townsend Harris*.

Bessie Harris had been careful to burn the volumes dated after February 27, 1858. But even the journal entries prior to that date, which were eventually published, contained several passages that point to Harris's cobang profiteering. Because the wording in these passages is rather vague, she must not have understood what they really meant. If she had, she would have never considered publication.

Harris had not foreseen that his journal would be published after his death. He thus did not revise the incriminating passages, and the world came to see him for what he was.